Crusher

Black Hawk MC
Book Two

by Carson Mackenzie

Published by CM Books, LLC
Copyright © April 2016 Carson Mackenzie
Cover Design by Carson Mackenzie
ISBN# 978-1-952184-27-7
ISBN# 978-1-078746-66-3
ISBN# 978-1-710318-00-5

Synopsis

Russ "Crusher" Davis will take over as president of Black Hawk MC when his father steps down. He realizes the job isn't going to be easy, but with his friends, the club's support, and the loyalty of its members behind him, there are no problems he can't solve.

Carly Monroe has been raised in one club and protected by another but has no trust in either. Club life may work for her friend; however, she has no plans to follow in her footsteps, not for Sami or for the man whose touch puts cracks in the wall she's built around her heart.

Crusher knows with a strong woman beside him, his impending presidency won't suffer—Black Hawk will thrive for future generations. Now all he has to do is show one woman that she doesn't have to be alone—friends, family, and the love of a good man are there if she will open her heart and embrace them.

Table of Contents

Prologue

Crusher

"Ten fucking minutes!" I yelled over the sound of my engine. Carly had a head start, but not that much. I left Speed's house and thought I would catch up to her on the road into town. No such luck. The girl could handle a bike, but not like I would admit that shit to her. Why I was even chasing her was beyond me, damn it, I needed to have my fucking head examined.

The first stop had been her apartment. After banging on the door until the neighbor yelled she had left about a minute before I showed up, only pissed me off. As soon as the woman shut her door, I proceeded to pick the lock. I hoped she left some kinda sign of where she was headed but oh no, not my girl. *My girl?* Christ, I had to be upset for that thought to surface. How the hell could I even consider her my girl? The woman hated the ground I walked on. She'd made that abundantly clear more than once.

I walked through the living room, which held the standard things: couch, chair, TV, and end tables. The kitchen, as I entered, had a few boxes sitting out with stuff packed in them. I knew she planned to move to Sami's house after Sami and Ally finished moving in with Speed. The place was neat and clean, organized just as I thought the woman would be. Carly was medium height and petite, and I was blown away the first time I came in contact with her. Her blond hair and big brown eyes would draw any man's attention, they did me, but after I introduced myself and spoke with her, the strength that exuded from her was what did me in. Women had always come easy for me, for all of us, as a matter of fact. Pulling out all the stops to entice a woman was an experience I only had once. It had been with her.

When I reached the bedroom door upstairs, I pushed it open to find the same as the rest of the apartment. The clothes thrown over the chair were the only sign it was a woman's room. If the others saw me pick up her tank top and hold it to my face, they'd laugh themselves silly, and the ribbing would start. Alone, standing in her space, her smell instantly brought peace to me, but it didn't scare or shock me. It had the same effect as the woman's touch had, the unrestrained passion I'd been lucky enough to witness and participate in, the one and only time I'd had her. I found nothing in her place to hint where she would go, so I laid the shirt down and left, locking the front door behind me. I got on my bike and headed to the sheriff's station, a place I would normally avoid at all cost, so that alone should have been a sign of how totally messed up this was.

"Hi ya, Russ. What brings you in here?" Shirley Sansom had worked at the sheriff's office since I'd been a kid.

"Hey, Shirley, you'll lookin' as good as ever, darlin'. When are you gonna dump old Erving and run away with me?" Shirley smiled hugely at me while her skin tinged the slightest pink at my words.

"Oh stop, you always were the most wicked one out of you boys. I swear, I don't think there's a woman in this town that doesn't swoon when one of you speaks," she chuckled. "What can I do for you, Russ?"

"I wish that were true. Seems to be one in this town that's immune to us, or at least to me. Deputy Monroe been by today?"

"No, was she expecting you? Haven't you seen her? She's been off the last few days helping Sami move. Did you try over at the house? Carly's going to move in there after Sami clears out."

"I knew that, except I forgot about her moving over to the house until I swung by her apartment. I'll go there. Thanks, Shirley." The door opened as I turned to leave, and Sheriff Lance walked in. "Sheriff."

"Russ. Tell me that you and my deputy aren't fighting again. What the hell is up with that shit?" Yeah, like I was going to get into that particular discussion with him.

"Nah, no issue with her."

"Good, glad you didn't have anything to do with her calling to ask for a few more days off. The girl doesn't ever take time for herself, so I'm glad to see her doing it."

"Huh? She took some more time?" So not good. "Did she happen to say where she was going?" I could tell the sheriff weighed if he should say more or not.

"Sorry, no. But I want to know why you are interested in my deputy taking time off. Other than her friend moving to Black Hawk, it's not like you're close to her." I ran my fingers through my hair, something which was still new to me since I'd been letting it grow out after coming out of the military. I might as well be honest with the man.

"She got some disquieting news. Took off from helping us settle Sami and Ally in at Speed's place. I followed to make sure she was alright."

"What kind of news?" I had no right to share it, even if he was the sheriff. Not like it was anything illegal that should concern him. This was personal and none of his business.

"If Carly wants you to know, I'm sure she will tell you. Not up to me." He was going to have to accept it, and from how the sheriff clenched his jaw, he was debating it with himself.

"I'll give you that for now. But I want you to remember that I've always supported the Black Hawk members. I went to school with your dad, and when he came back here with his buddies from the service, I was glad to see him. The club set up businesses here, they pay taxes here, and they support the local community. I've watched you six boys grow up along with several of the members' children, but I will come down on the lot of you if you hurt that girl. She moved here, went to college, got her criminal justice degree, and applied when a position opened after John Talbot got injured badly in a car accident and had to resign. I've watched her grow into a fine deputy from the first time she wore the uniform. I'm giving you the heads up so you'll know I would do *anything* in my power to keep her safe." He held his hand up when I went to speak, cutting me off and continuing, "I can see it in your eyes, Russ. You were going to remind me she came from an MC and was sent here for the club to watch over. I know that. I also know she doesn't care too much about either club. The girl is strong-willed. Some of it is just a tough front too. I don't know what happened in her life to make her overly guarded when it comes to certain things, and I'm not going to guess at the other things, either. So I'm going to ask, are we clear on her?"

The man could never be accused of being stupid, he'd keyed right in on her just as I had. There's a lot to Carly, it'd take the right person to peel back the layers, and though I never gave a shit before about digging deep into what makes a chick click, I have to admit with her—I want to know it all—I need to.

"Going to drive by Sami's old place, see if she is there. Need to find her. If you hear from her again, will you let us know and see if she'll tell you where she is?"

"Carly's not at the house. I went by after she called me to see if I could talk with her in person. She sounded as if she was a little upset, but when I asked, she was adamant that she was fine. Her truck is parked in the driveway, so she's on her bike. I'll let you get on your way without telling me what is going on with her, but you better damn well keep me up-to-date." He grabbed his messages off Shirley's desk and headed toward his office without another word. I looked toward Shirley, and she shrugged.

Nothing else needed to be said, so I turned and left. Carly had a good head start on me now, but considering I didn't know where she was headed, I needed to take my ass back to Black Hawk and regroup.

When I stopped my bike in front of Speed's house, he and Sami stepped out on the porch.

"Have you heard from her?" I asked as I got off my bike and headed toward them.

"Nah, Sami's called her cell a dozen times, texted her, and left voicemail messages. Nothing," Speed replied.

"Any idea where she would go, Sami?" I stepped up on the porch.

"I called my dad, Haven's the only place she would go, but he hasn't heard from her. Said he would call if he did."

"You doing okay, brother, had a bomb dropped on you?" Speed nodded and put his arm around Sami, drawing her close.

"Yeah, I'm good, brother. Carly should've stayed and talked with me. No way could she think I knew about her being related to me and kept quiet about it. And I got questions of my own, like what the hell Stone thought he would gain contacting Cutter. On another note, Carly was lucky, it looks like Clarice found a home at Haven and stayed with one of her kids. Still doesn't answer why he'd want to talk with Cutter over a dead druggy, even if Cutter and he both had been involved with her. Makes no sense." Speed furrowed his brows.

"Kane, I'm not sure Carly would agree with that," Sami said and looked between the both of us.

"What is that supposed to mean, Sami?" Speed looked down at Sami.

"I'm not sure what all happened, Speed. Carly was never one to talk about her home life."

"Why the hell not?" I asked.

"Figure it out, Crusher. Her parents were drug users, Clarice was an addict, and although Stone was a sometimes user, he stuck more with booze. We don't get to choose our parents, so we shouldn't have to pay for their crimes, but I feel Carly feels guilty because of Stone's betrayal of the club." Sami leaned her head on Speed's shoulder.

"That's bullshit. Is that where some of her intolerance for MCs comes from? Her fucked up parents are not the standard in clubs. She should have known that from watching the other members at Haven."

"Crusher, I don't know why she feels that way; it hadn't always been like that with her. When we moved here, she had already been talking about building a life that didn't include any part of an MC. I wish I knew more, but I don't. She wouldn't talk about it other than to say that her experience hadn't been like mine," Sami said, and Speed pulled her tighter to him.

"Could it be why she took off when she found out I was her half-brother?" Speed asked. "I'm in a club, and she doesn't want that anymore?"

"Not sure, but we need to figure this out. Did you speak with Stroker while I was gone?" Speed shook his head no. "Might as well wait. He and the others are due back late tonight. We can get with them in the morning, show them the note and see what they might remember from that time. Until we speak with Carly, I guess we wait. Did you get everything unloaded into the house?"

"Yeah, Devil and Flirt went to turn in the truck. Jag and Coast walked over to Shakes and Dare's place to retrieve Ally for us."

"Well, if you don't need me to help with anything else, I think I'm going to head to the house, shower, get something to eat, and hit the bed. Call me if you hear from Carly. I'd like to know she's alright." I turned and headed back to my bike.

"Crusher?" I looked back at Speed when my name was called. "Why are you so interested in Carly's wellbeing?" Sami elbowed him, and he looked down at her, "What? It's a good question. He runs out after her, worries about where she's gone, and then searches for her. He acts like he's fuc—" Sami cut Speed off before he could finish.

"Kane Weston, do not finish that sentence. And stop interrogating Crusher. What's between them is their business."

"Sami, you know something I don't?" Speed glared at her.

"Ugh, you are unbelievable. I'm going in to fix something to eat, Ally will be back soon." Sami turned and walked into the house. I straddled the bike and revved it, pulling Speed's attention from watching his woman's ass as she disappeared from sight.

"Hey, I'm not done talking with you! You didn't answer my question," he yelled over the sound of the bike.

I pointed the bike in my house's direction. "I sure didn't," I yelled as I rode past him to my house, which really didn't sit that far away from Speed's.

"Asshole!" Speed yelled no sooner than I stopped my bike in front of my house. I flipped him off and walked in. *It was probably going to be one long-ass sleepless night*, I thought as I kicked the door shut behind me.

Chapter One

Carly

The ride had been long and boring by myself, but the wind and the open road had cleared my head, as it always did. Learning to ride was one of the few enjoyments of MC life that I had had. I bought my first new bike when I was hired as a deputy. It wasn't one of the decked-out bikes, but my Softail Slim fit me nicely, and the monthly payment was low enough that I could still afford to eat between rent and utilities. My truck was compliments of Wild Bill, his excuse was I needed a vehicle to get back and forth to college. I know he felt obligated because of sending Sami and me to Black Hawk territory, but it didn't make me feel good since my dad had been the reason he had to do it in the first place.

The note had shocked me but shouldn't have ridden off as I did. No, it had been a rash, dumb move. When I'd checked the pocket of the leather jacket, found the paper, and unfolded it to see what it was—my world had shifted a little, and I'd panicked when I'd seen who'd written it, more so than what it revealed. I could remember every word on it.

> *Cutter,*
> *Meet me in town, I have info on something that belongs to Black Hawk you might want. You help me out, maybe I'll let you know what it is. If nothing else, we can compare notes on Clarice. You got stuck with the son, and I got stuck with the daughter.*
> *I'll be waiting for you,*
>
> *Stone*

Halfway through the trip, I stopped feeling sorry for myself about having two parents who, if I was lucky, forgot they even had a child. Then I thought of Speed and how if I'd known or he had known, would we have had any contact? All the days, I'd sat in my room in that crappy trailer and wished I had a sibling to play with, someone to talk to.

Sami had been my solace growing up. And even though I never shared the things I witnessed in my house or dealt with, I always felt she'd understood anyway. As we got older, more and more she invited me to stay at her house. I'd mourned more when her mother died than I had my own.

Wild Bill was president of Haven, but he seemed to have more time for his family than Stone, the club's VP, had for his. Sami's parents never treated me as anything other than part of their family. Their house was where I learned how a family should interact. Even Reed treated me like another sister.

With just a quarter of the trip left, I decided that now was the time to get over the shit I had no control over. I wasn't responsible for my mother being a whore or for Stone plotting to take over Haven. My past was what molded me into the grown woman I am. No matter how hard I tried to push away, the Haven MC was a part of me—good, bad, or indifferent.

The fence leading to the clubhouse came into view, and I took a deep breath. The gates were folded open with a couple of prospects standing guard. I stopped my bike and waited for them to approach. Since I didn't know who the men were, meant they didn't know me, and no one just drove onto Haven property. Well, unless you had a death wish. Some tended to shoot and ask questions later.

"Hey, sugar, you here to relieve us?" I rolled my eyes, then furrowed my brow as he looked me over and licked his lips. I wasn't that old, so the guy in front of me was probably just recently out of his pimple stage. I hoped he had better pickup lines in his arsenal because that one sucked, and he would never get laid, even by the hang-arounds.

"I'm here to see the Prez." I'd called about five minutes ago and spoke to Wild Bill to let him know I was headed in and thought maybe he would have notified whoever was at the gate. Why would I be that lucky after the day I had? Wild Bill had been upset about me traveling alone, especially with Stone and a couple of friends in the wind. Sami had already called her dad, and Wild Bill informed me we would talk after I arrived.

"Ah, a new piece for Prez, huh? He'll get tired of you, and then we can have a spin with you." The other prospect stood there but never spoke. I looked between them, and my conclusion was, yeah, the non-talker was the smarter one. Not only had I not wanted to think of Wild Bill having sex, I definitely didn't want to be part of the scene either, considering he was like a father to me.

"Dipshit, do you have a cellphone? Want to use mine, if you don't?" I reached behind to grab my cell phone out of the pocket of my jeans, it slipped, I bobbled it and then caught it right before it would have hit the ground. The movement had me bent over the side of the bike, and before I could rise, I heard the click of a gun's magazine being snapped into place. Well, I didn't need to guess that my jacket must have risen up in the back and revealed my gun.

"Could the day get any freakin' better?" I mumbled.

"Sit up, bitch. Sparks, call this in. Make sure to inform them she was asking about the Prez."

Okay, maybe he wasn't the slow one of the two. Out of the corner of my eye, across the parking lot, the door to the clubhouse opened just as Sparks pulled out his phone.

"What the hell are you doing, Taylor?!" Reed yelled as he headed toward us.

"Bitch asked for Prez, and she's carrying."

I didn't move even with Reed getting closer. I wasn't about to give the guy a reason to pull the trigger.

"You were told she was on her way in. And put your damn gun down. Carly is a part of this club, dumbshit."

"We didn't get told, Keg." I'd almost forgotten Reed had a club name until the guy used it. Sami and I never called him by it, he'd always been Reed to us.

"Mondo didn't call either of you?" Reed asked.

"No, Keg, neither one of us received the message," the one I assumed was Taylor answered.

"Okay, carry on. Carly, meet me at the door. Prez has been waiting for you."

"You got it," I answered, then looked at Taylor, "And, next time, dipshit, when you pull a gun on me, don't wait to use it. I don't wear one for show." I hit the throttle and moved into the parking lot without a backward glance.

By the time I backed my bike into a spot and threw my leg over to get off, Reed walked up.

"He's pissed you rode here by yourself. So good luck with that. It was a stupid move on your part, Carly."

"I wasn't thinking when I pulled out, Reed. Don't give me any shit. Plus, I can take care of myself."

"Do you think someone coming after you is going to carry a damn sign or walk up to you? They're not. They'll hit you when you least expect it, and you won't have enough time to think about what is going on before they have you." Reed started toward the door. "You've always been stubborn, I'd forgotten that." Reed pulled the door open and held it, letting me enter before him. As I crossed the threshold, my stomach flipped. It was my first time back to the place where I had spent almost every day for the first eighteen years of my life. The men who sat in the main room were my family.

"Well goddamn, look who decided to come back to town. What's up, mouse?" The tall, bulky man with dirty blond hair approached me. To say I was surprised to see him at the Haven's clubhouse would have been an understatement. He was a fucking prick. I grew up with him, and there was no love loss between us. My eyes narrowed when I looked at him. He was a disgrace. How the hell he had even become part of the Haven MC was beyond me.

"Gavin. Did Haven have a pity drive for members? Or did they get an EO complaint about not letting any women become actual members, so you were the closest thing to one they could come up to meet the criteria?" His face morphed, and his eyes flashed with instant anger at my words. He'd always had a temper growing up, especially when he didn't get his way. I should know. I had been on the receiving end of that nasty piece of work a few times. Hell, he was lucky I hadn't kicked his ass back then and embarrassed the shit out of him.

"Brother, you were fucking supposed to inform Taylor and Sparks that Carly was on her way in?" Reed spoke, gathering Gavin's attention.

"I called. The punks didn't answer their cells. I was on my way down there, but you walked in with her." I hoped, like hell, Reed didn't believe his lying ass. He had always been easy to read, at least, that hadn't changed.

"Oh yeah, I'll take a look at their phones later and see if your number shows. And if you are lying, I will take action a different way, one you won't like. We clear?" Reed gave him the look Sami, and I received too many times to count for getting caught spying on him when he was with a girl or when he would catch us in his room looking at the magazines he had hidden under his bed. He wasn't that much older than us, but when you were girls who started to get breasts and noticed boys, we'd figured if we watched him and the things he did, we would be one up on all the girls our age.

"Fuck, Keg, alright, I didn't get a chance to call them. I had to take a shit right after you told me to notify them. I just came out of the bathroom and was on my way to the gate."

"When I tell you to do something, I expect it done then, not at your fucking convenience. You gotta go to the john, do it after my orders. This isn't the first time you've not followed orders, but it will be the last. Next time you'll be begging for mercy by the time I am done with you. Got it, Mondo." Gavin's head nodded in agreement with Reed, but his eyes shined with defiance, and I could see the hatred buried deep in them. He did not like getting reprimanded openly in front of the members present in the room or me. I knew I shouldn't add fuel to the fire, but my dislike for Gavin overrode my better judgment.

"Mondo? Seriously?" I chuckled, bringing Gavin's gaze back to me, and he smirked.

"Yeah, mouse, 'cause of the size of my dick." Gavin grabbed his crotch, and I couldn't help myself, and I burst out laughing.

"Oh please, let's not get carried away here. Don't forget, I've seen it. When you tried to get me to touch it the day in the trailer park, I was like ten, and you were what? Fourteen. I don't think it could have grown that much since then." The smirk left his face, and the glare I received just seconds ago returned, and anger blazed in his eyes. I should have known when I saw the look in his eyes, but honest to God, I figured he was too pussy to do a damn thing.

He reached out, and his hand grabbed my throat. I knew that being unable to keep my mouth shut would lead to problems someday. Of course, I had my own temper issues, so I quickly grabbed his junk and squeezed. The hand on my throat released as quickly as it had latched on, and the fucker instantly dropped to his knees as I twisted his package with one hand and had my gun out with the other, aiming at his head. I had grown up a lot since the trailer park, and he had mistaken me for actually giving two shits about his sorry ass ego.

"Holy shit," was yelled from a couple of the men in the room as I glared back at Gavin.

"Carly put the gun away and let go of Mondo's damn cock." Reed had moved closer to me.

"Well, Jesus Christ, Carly! Even time away doesn't seem to have changed shit. Just once, I would like to see you enter my clubhouse and not start any crap."

I turned my head and smiled at Wild Bill. Then I let go of Gavin's dick and tucked my gun back into the waist of my pants, "Ah, I was just congratulating Gavin on being a member of Haven, Wild Bill."

"Come over here and give me a hug, girl. It wouldn't kill you to show some respect in my clubhouse and call me Prez." He opened up his arms and smiled, and I moved into them. He'd showed me more love in my life than my own dad.

"You got it, Wild Bill," I grinned as I hugged him back.

"Smartass," he whispered in my ear, and I hugged him a little tighter.

"What the hell, the bitch comes in here, insults and pulls a gun on a patched member, and no one does fucking shit," Gavin said, and when I released Wild Bill and turned around, Reed was in his face. The idiot had not fucking learned.

"The key word is patched member. Carly was born into this fucking club. You, Mondo, were accepted in and earned a patch, but, motherfucker, the patch can be taken just as easily as it was given. You know, like for not following my fucking orders! Stop acting like a pussy, take your ass down to the gate, and relieve the prospects so they can get something to eat. And next time you put your hands on her, I'll let her ass shoot you." Gavin stomped out, and Reed walked toward Wild Bill and me. "Want me to bring some food for you and Carly to your office, Prez?" Reed asked calmly as if he hadn't just reamed someone's ass.

27

"Oh my God, you really are an enforcer in the club?" I knew he had earned the position after the shit my dad had caused with his backstabbing treachery, but I'd never seen him in full enforcer mode.

"What the fucked did you think I was?"

"Don't get all indignant, Reed. Pull your panties out of their wad. It hit me that you have grown up, and Sami and I missed it. That's all."

He actually rolled his eyes at me, "Carly, fuck, I'm older than you, dumbass. And it's not like you haven't seen me when I come down with Prez to visit."

"Alright, let's move this party to my office so you can tell us what brought you hightailing it here, and then I can fix it." Wild Bill put his arm around my shoulders and turned me toward his office. "Reed, grab the food and some drinks and join us."

"Sure thing, Prez," Reed responded and headed in the opposite direction.

As I walked down the hallway, the emotions about why I was here hit me. I'd panicked over a damn piece of paper. Avoidance was my specialty, and damn it, right about now, with the door to Wild Bill's office getting closer and closer, I was kicking my own ass for coming here. Was I ready to hear what I suspected? Hell, did I even want to freaking listen to what the truth was?

"Okay, sit and start talking." Wild Bill closed the door to his office as soon as we walked in.

Why did I suddenly feel five?

Chapter Two

Carly

Wild Bill sat in his chair behind the desk and waited. *Where to begin?* I took a deep breath and started with what had me running back to Haven.

"Did you know? Is that why you moved me with Sami to their territory?" I asked.

"About Speed being your half-brother? No. I moved you with Sami because I didn't want Stone or anyone who was backing his takeover of this club to use you against me, Carly, you know that." I blew my breath out. I hadn't realized how much I needed his answer to be just that.

"Why would Stone want to meet with Speed's dad? What could he have that belongs to Black Hawk?" I knew there were things he wouldn't tell me because it would have to do with club business, but I asked anyway.

"Carly, I will tell you as much as I can to answer any of your questions, but are you really here to learn all the dark secrets of Haven MC? I've never known you to run from anything, even when you were small." Wild Bill's eyebrow lifted in question.

"I'm trying to understand, and I am coming up blank. I have my birth certificate. The section that is for other living children is blank on mine. Which means it's fake or has been altered. What would Clarice have gained by not telling me? It's not like she or Stone gave a shit, so why hide a half-brother? And he was setting things up to oust you and take over this club, but instead of kicking me out, you paid for my college, gave me a truck, and treated me like a daughter. I know you caught shit from some of the other members for it. You would have had to have." I'd worked hard not to be like either of my parents, and I knew I had succeeded, but those old insecurities would push through just when I thought I'd put it all behind me.

The door opened, and Reed walked in carrying a tray with drinks and sandwiches on it. After he had set it down on Wild Bill's desk, he pulled up a chair, and I slid mine closer. Wild Bill set a plate and drink in front of me and gave a chin lift toward the food, signaling for me to eat. I started eating, as did he and Reed, and after a few bites and taking a drink, Wild Bill settled back in his chair.

"Until I talked with Sami, I hadn't even known Clarice had any association with Black Hawk. I wish I knew more about her. She came to Haven with Stone when he returned from a run. My dad was still in charge of the club then, and Stone was newly voted in as VP. The word going around at the time had been she'd been whor…umm…hanging around at the Kings, she'd only been with them a couple of days. Stone got attached to her and brought her back with him. He made her his ol' lady, and not long after that, she was pregnant with you. I had just come out of the military then, Reed was barely school age, and my Ana was pregnant with Sami." Wild Bill stopped talking to take a drink.

"So you didn't know her well then. What about after? Did she ever mention another child in all the years here?" I pushed my plate away and sat back in my chair, my appetite gone.

"No, she never did. But, Carly, I'm trying to tell you that you aren't the first to want something different from an MC life. I left for the military at my dad's disapproval. I was raised in the Haven MC, my mother never married my dad, but she was his ol' lady. I stayed after she died. My dad needed me. I didn't think I would ever come back but to visit. Even when my dad was shot on that run, and I took the club over, I didn't know if I would stay, but now, I can't imagine being anywhere else." Wild Bill smiled at me.

"What about you, Reed? You've never left here. Did you ever want something else?" I asked him, he hadn't said a word since he'd been in the room.

"No, not once. I never wanted to be anywhere else."

"It's different for me," I said. Now, not only did I have ties to Haven, I had ties to Black Hawk because of Speed.

"How so, Carly? And don't say because women aren't part of the club other than club ass because all that does is insult every ol' lady." Wild Bill glared at me.

"I wasn't going to say that. I don't know why I came here." I looked down at my hands, I wasn't going to get any answers. Stone was running, and Clarice was dead.

"Bullshit," Reed said and slammed his hand down on Wild Bill's desk. I snapped my eyes to him. "Yeah, that there look, you had that out there," he pointed in the direction of the common room, "Christ, you pulled your damn gun on Mondo, Carly. Shit, girl, growing up, you were tougher than some of the prospects. You jumped on my bike at fifteen after I told you not to, and you rode that Fat Boy like you'd been on one all your life. You and Sami left here at eighteen, lived in a strange place, went to college, and only had each other. You never let Stone's and Clarice's actions hold you back then, so why the fuck would you start now? So you share blood with Speed. Are you worried he won't accept you? And don't say you shouldn't have come here. Haven is your damn home." Reed glared at me, and I glared back while Wild Bill watched us both.

"Goddamn, you two are so much alike. Thank fuck you didn't get together."

"Ewww," was said simultaneously as Reed and I turned toward Wild Bill.

"Got your attention real quick with that shit, didn't I?" Wild Bill chuckled, then continued. "I know you haven't been involved with anything to do with Black Hawk since you moved there. Sami said you and Stroker's son go head to head all the time, and your first time visiting her at Speed's house was to help with the move." Wild Bill cocked his brow, waiting for me to answer.

"Sami talks too much." I glared at Wild Bill. I wasn't ready to deal with the Crusher issue. It was bad enough that he haunted my dreams the last six months, and it didn't help that he would show up at the most impromptu times when I was close to forcing him out. He was strong and confident, and I was sure he would have no problem going after what he wanted. None of the ones I met would let anything stand in their way. I put up the wall between him and me, and so far, it was staying in place, but what would I do if he came at me as Speed had done with Sami? Then again, why would he want a woman whose dad was the one to ramrod a plot to take over the Haven MC? Crusher would be president one day, did he think Black Hawk members would accept me as his ol' lady? And why the hell was I even thinking about that shit? I never wanted to be club ass nor an ol' lady in any MC. If I had, I would have settled in at Haven. It wasn't like I never had interest shown to me.

"Are you worried about Speed accepting you? Is that it? Or is it you don't want to get to know him? You're going to be around him a lot if you're going to see Sami and Ally."

I know Reed was right, but I had tried to distance myself from MC life when in reality, to do it, I would have to give up the people I cared about the most. And I sure wouldn't have returned to Haven, though there I sat.

"No, maybe."

"What kind of damn answer is that? Family, Carly. That is what it is all about, and it has nothing to do with the blood that runs through your veins but everything to do with who accepts you unconditionally, no matter what. And if you think you aren't worthy because of the shit Stone's pulled, I should kick your ass." Reed stood, gathered up the dishes, and placed them back on the tray. He was right again, but no way would I admit that to him. Hell, he'd never let me live it down, even if we lived to be a hundred.

"Yeah, you can try. What makes you think I wouldn't shoot *your* ass?" He stood, holding the tray, and looked at me. The smirk followed, and then he laughed.

Wild Bill, who had listened and watched the exchange, stood. "Whoever said maturity comes with age, never had to deal with you guys. Let's head to my house and get you settled in a room, Carly. Fucked up shit may be what brought you here, but it's still good to have you back, even if only for a few days."

"We'll see if you still feel that way by the time I get ready to leave." We laughed and headed out the office door. I really had missed Wild Bill. Even Reed.

When we walked into the common room, a few of Haven's men who were hanging around at the bar yelled for Wild Bill to come over. As we neared, I recognized a few of them, they'd been here before I left, and the patches on their cuts showed that a change had occurred by my father's betrayal. Sami and I were never told what had gone down, only that the club was getting cleaned up.

"Hey, Carly, you remember Hawk, Moose, and Pinch, don't you?" Wild Bill asked.

"Sure do, Prez. And I see Haven voted in some top quality officers." I winked at the men as they shook their heads and laughed.

"Damn, I'm taking this tray back to the kitchen. Shit in here is getting deep," Reed grumbled and walked away.

"Fuckin' A, Prez. I was told we had a cop in the clubhouse, and I had to see for myself because no cop is ever at Haven unless they're picking up on a warrant." Hawk was a prospect around the same time as the others. He was the first true crush I had. He hadn't changed much other than the short blond hair cut close to his scalp showed the slightest bit of gray at his temples. Now Hawk wore the patch signifying he was now Haven's VP, making him the replacement for my dad, Stone.

"But, man, if the cops around here looked like you, I wouldn't mind getting cuffed." Moose's eyes traveled the length of my body. I rolled my eyes at him. Tall, dark, and handsome as sin, and I felt not one ounce of a draw to him.

"When did you get out, Moose?" I asked. He'd gone to prison right before Sami, and I left Haven. I'd known it had to do with something for the club but never knew the exact reason. Club business was club business.

"Only did a couple of years, no biggie, anything for Haven." Wild Bill patted Moose's shoulder, and I didn't miss the looks exchanged between the men. As a deputy, I wanted to question them, but sometimes it was better not to know.

"You boys stay out of trouble. Hawk, text me when the men come back from the run. I'm taking Carly to the house to get her settled if you need me. If not, I'll see you tomorrow." The guys nodded, then Reed walked up, and the three of us left. I mounted my bike and waited for them to do the same, and as we pulled out of the lot, my decision to come here felt right for the first time since I left Black Hawk territory.

A few days at Haven, getting my head together, could be just what I needed.

Chapter Three

Crusher

As I sat on the porch drinking my coffee, the sun was cresting the top of the mountains. Sleeping through the night was a distant luxury I hadn't experienced in a while. When I'd come home yesterday, I had showered, eaten dinner, and tried to relax by watching some TV. Nothing worked. The only text I'd gotten was from my dad, letting me know they'd arrived home. After I layed down and closed my eyes, a blonde kept popping into my head. Had she made it to Haven? Hell, had she even gone to Haven?

At one point, I'd tossed and turned so much that I thought about going to the garage to work on one of the bike orders. I would have if the garage didn't sit behind Speed's house. I didn't want to disturb Sami and Ally.

My phone buzzed. Pulling it out of my pocket, I looked down to see private caller on the screen, it made the tenth call in two weeks that came through like that. I clicked the talk button to answer, "Russ," then the same as the last time. Nothing, followed by the disconnect sound. Fucking shit was annoying, and I was going to have to have Coast see if he could trace it. If nothing else but to get whoever it was to stop calling me.

After going in and placing the coffee cup in the sink, I headed to the bathroom, off my bedroom, stripping along the way. My face in the mirror had me stopping in front of it, and I didn't like what I saw. My blue eyes showed the fatigue I felt throughout my body, and the stubble on my face showed the three days' worth of growth I hadn't bothered to shave off. The stubble could stay, but another hot shower was warranted to help wash the fatigue away. I noticed lately how Stroker watched me, though he hadn't said a word to me about it or asked any questions, I knew it was only a matter of time.

I turned the knobs to start the water in the shower while I brushed my teeth, waiting for it to heat up. Once the steam began to rise, I stepped in to let the water attempt to rejuvenate me. I placed my hands on the wall and bent my head under the water, letting it rain down over my head and slide down my body while I ran over every piece of info we had, which wasn't much. Hopefully, whenever Carly got back, we'd get more to add to it. Carly. Damn it, I couldn't kick her out of my head, at least not as easily as she kicked me out of her bed. I removed one hand from the wall to slide it down my chest, over my abs, until I reached my straining cock. Never fucking failed; the thought of her, arguing with her, or just having her glare at me as I passed by gave me a hard-on.

With my hand wrapped around my cock, I closed my eyes and pictured how Carly woke me the morning after we'd spent the night together.

My eyes opened to see her head bobbing on my cock. The feeling of her tongue as she licked the underside from root to tip, circling her tongue around the head and then working my length back in her mouth until my dick touched the back of her throat. I'd only laid still for a couple of swipes before my hand went into her hair, and I wrapped it around to control her motions. Her eyes met mine and held as I moved her head up and down on my dick.

"Don't you dare gag. Breathe through your nose and take it all. That's it." My hips bucked as I brought her head down, and when I pulled her up, she hollowed her cheeks, sucking me hard as my cock slipped from her mouth till just the tip remained. Her tongue swiped the slit and my hips bucked.

"Let me, Russ." Her voice was husky, and her lips were swollen as she waited. I released her hair and placed my hands behind my head on the pillow.

"All yours, darlin'," was all I got out before she engulfed my cock, and when she swallowed, taking me further down her throat, my hands moved from behind my head to latch onto the sheets.

She moaned around my cock, and I felt the beginning of my orgasm with the vibration. I tried to pull her off. Instead, she placed a hand at the base to hold my dick steady as worked me.

"You better be ready to swallow," I ground out, she sucked hard, and I emptied my load down her throat.

"Fuck." I slapped the wall, and my eyes shot open as I stroked myself to the finish. I washed off, got out of the shower, toweled my body off, and headed into the bedroom.

In the prior months, every time I thought of that morning, it pissed me off more. We'd been fuckin' awesome together, but when we'd lain back on the bed that morning, she curled into my arms as we talked, and it didn't take long for it all to go to hell. I'd told her that I wanted to see her again, get to know her, and spend some time together. I thought she lived in Moorehead, she thought I did. She'd shaken her head and laughed, told me she was a deputy in Shades Valley. I'd laughed too and told her I hadn't been back but a couple of weeks, that I lived outside of Shades Valley out at the Black Hawk MC compound. I never saw anyone move that quick out of bed, never. And frankly, I should know, not once since I joined the military had I stayed the night with a woman. Carly had been the first. It didn't get past me that I hadn't woken during the night with cold sweats either.

"Damn, were you jacking off in the shower? I thought I was going to have to go get my wetsuit and save you from drowning." Flirt was sitting in the corner chair with his feet propped up on the stool in front of it, a smirk on his face.

"Fuck you." I walked into the closet, pulled on a pair of jeans, then walked back out, tucking in my junk before zipping.

"Nah, I'm good." Flirt stood.

"Why is your ass in my bedroom?" I asked, grabbing a t-shirt out of a drawer and pulling it on.

"Stroker wants us over at the clubhouse. Check your phone, he called, and you didn't answer." Flirt opened his arms wide, then continued. "That is why you got me." I picked the phone off the dresser, and sure enough, there was the text asking where the fuck are you and a missed call, along with one from Speed.

"The others already head over?"

"Yep, they caught me before I left the house to ask me to stop by since you hadn't replied."

"Let's go then. We walking or riding over?"

"Walk. I could use the exercise," Flirt said as he walked out of the bedroom. The walk to the clubhouse would only take about five minutes.

The TV was blaring when we walked into the clubhouse, and the only occupant in the room sat on the couch with her head bent down. I pulled on the ponytail hanging off the back of her head as Flirt, and I stood behind her.

"What ya doing out here by yourself, Spider?" She glanced away from the phone she had been playing on to look over her shoulder.

"Watching cartoons. Momma told me not to move until she came back."

41

It was still strange having Speed's eyes looking back at me. Ally looked so much like him, he could have been the one to pop her out if it was been possible.

"Where is your momma, sweetheart?"

"With Daddy in Papa Stroker's office." She bent her head back over the phone while I stood there with a smile spreading across my face. I looked at Flirt, and he just shrugged. The girl was too cute for her own good, and it hadn't taken her but a few days to wrap some of the hardest men I'd known around her tiny fingers, including me.

"Papa Stroker, huh?" I couldn't wait to hear how that came about.

"Uh huh. All my papas are in there, too. 'Cept Papa Wild Bill, he lives away." Not once as she answered did she turn back to look at us. Spider was going to be a handful as she grew up. I didn't envy Speed and Sami, or myself for that matter, considering I would be the president of the club when she hit her teens. Damn, I didn't want to go there until I had to. Shaking the thought away, I turned toward the office, Flirt right behind me.

"Don't go anywhere until your momma comes and gets you, okay?" I yelled a reminder over my shoulder.

"'K," was the reply just as we reached the office, then replaced loud voices from behind the door.

"Calm down, Speed. We hung the jacket in the closet when we received his things from the coroner's office after the accident."

I knocked once and pushed open the office door. The room was full of my friends, the dads, and Sami, who was sitting on the couch that was against the wall with Coast and Jag. The others sat in chairs. My dad, Stroker, stopped talking when Flirt and I entered, causing everyone to turn and look at us.

"You stop answering your phone?" Stroker asked.

"I was in the shower and didn't hear it," I answered and walked over to stand by my dad's desk as Flirt took an empty chair.

Speed looked ready to combust if the redness from his neck up to his face was any indication. I figured he was about five seconds away from total combustion.

"Did you hear anything from her?" I asked.

"She's at Haven," all eyes turned toward Sami as soon as the words left her mouth.

"How do you know that?" I asked.

"She didn't call. My dad did. He didn't go into any detail about what she said when she arrived there. He was just letting me know she was safe."

"I asked you to call me if you heard from her. I would have liked to have had the information." Stroker turned at my tone, and Speed glared at me.

"It was late, brother. You're hearing it now," Speed said. A warning blazing shooting from his eyes let me know he didn't appreciate my tone with Sami.

"I still do not understand why she would go there by herself. Isn't that why Wild Bill moved you and her here, to keep you away from the club?" It made no sense to me.

"Seriously, don't yell at my woman, brother. She's trying to help with this, and Carly is her friend." I would've laughed at the fierceness pouring off Speed if this situation weren't serious. The brother was a goner, and it hadn't taken that long either. I didn't know which way I leaned more: happy that my best friend had a family of his own now or envy for the peace that usually showed in his eyes, something I wondered if I would ever experience again after leaving the military.

"Sorry, Sami. I'm just pissed I couldn't catch up with Carly yesterday, and I didn't mean to yell at you." She smiled in acknowledgment, but it didn't reach full force. I knew she was worried for her friend.

"Before you got here, we were discussing why Cutter wouldn't have said anything about Clarice being at Haven and hooked up with the VP there, Wallace "Stone" Monroe." Speed looked at me, then at my dad.

"As I said, we didn't know about it. We'd heard she went to another club, but that was it. We never thought any more about it until news reached us about her overdose. Which, if I had to guess, Cutter just got that paper and headed into town, not bothering to tell us shit before he left."

"Bullshit, Dad wouldn't have run out the goddamn house because some piece of shit sent him a paper stating Clarice was whoring it up over at Haven and Cutter should come to town so they could sit down and chat about the whore they had shared."

Yeah, my buddy was wound tight.

"Makes her your half-sister, Speed—" He cut me off before I was finished.

"As if I don't fucking know, yeah Carly is my half-sister, but that doesn't answer why Cutter got the fucking note. That fucker from Haven is on the run and has been for close to five years. Who knows what he's up to. If he was in town, don't you think he would have stopped in and seen his daughter? Sami swears Haven doesn't know anything other than he tried to take over Haven. They didn't know he'd figured out she and Carly were here. I question why after eighteen years, he decided to drop that shit of Clarice and having something that belonged to Black Hawk. Fucker couldn't have been talking about Clarice, and if he had been, why fucking wait? Something doesn't sit right because if it had been just to rub Dad's nose in the fact that Clarice was his ol' lady, the asshole would have done it when Clarice hooked up with him. Now we need to figure out why he felt Cutter was the one to go to. Clarice was dead a couple of years by that time, not like she was alive, and he expected Cutter to sit down and share stories on a woman they each had screwed. None of the shit makes sense."

"As I was saying, she's your sister, man. And if the prick was in our territory, she didn't know that. No way she knew anything until today when she came across that damn paper. Her face went pale, and her eyes were huge and tear-filled." I knew Speed was running every possible scenario through his head, each ending with the same conclusion—why contact Cutter?

"Yeah, but why run out? I was in the next room. Why not question me, or bitch about the shit? I realize she doesn't know me, but if all this is true, then we share a mother, well, an incubator, because the bitch was never a mother to me." Sami got up, walked over to Speed, and wrapped her arms around his waist. He took a deep breath, and I watched him physically relax in her arms. As I watched them whisper to each other, my resolve to have that became clearer than the target through the scope of my sniper's rifle ever had. No matter what it took, I always hit my target. The situation might be different, but the outcome would be the same—I'd locked in. Now I just needed to hit the mark. Difference— instead of eliminating, I wanted to possess.

"So why we try to piece all this shit together, what are we planning to do? The asshole is riding in the wind with a couple of his flunkies. Who knows where he is, but my gut says Carly shouldn't be alone." All eyes turned to me.

"Sami, will Wild Bill call when she gets ready to head back here?" Stroker spoke to Sami, but his eyes were still watching me. I know he was wondering why I was so interested in finding Sami's friend.

"Yes, he said he would, Stroker. We haven't left this town since the day we moved here. The farthest we traveled was over to Morehead to attend community college classes. My dad stressed to us about keeping a low profile, it's why he came here to visit. He didn't want us around the mess he was trying to clean up at Haven, nor did he want us near the members until he could clear them as being a threat. He's still unsure if he has weeded them all out." I ran my hand through my hair, stopping when I reached the back of my neck to rub it as I listened to Sami answer.

"Okay," Stroker said and looked around at each of us. No one had breathed a word, they sat quietly and listened. When I wasn't stressed, I'd think about the fact no one spoke or interrupted. It had to be some kinda fucking record. "We are going to have to wait for Carly to call or show back up. I know some of you aren't going to like that option," he paused and looked directly at me, "but deal with it. I will check in with Sheriff Lance to see if he remembers anything strange going on around town or if any unknown bikers had been spotted in town around the time of Cutter's accident. Speed, we need verification she's your half-sister. It will be the first step to finding out what the hell is going on in Black Hawk territory. We've gotten too comfortable. Maybe a little too relaxed with what happens in our town." Stroker held up his hand to stop Speed from interrupting him, "We need to know exactly what we are dealing with. Stone had his sights on Haven. What advantage was he looking to gain by bringing Black Hawk into his shit back then." Speed nodded his agreement with Stroker. I knew my friend had his own issues with finding out he still had a blood relative in this world, even if it wasn't confirmed yet. But I couldn't stop the uneasy feeling about Carly being on her own.

"I can't sit tight waiting for her to fucking come back. What if she's in danger at Haven? How the fuck are we going to help her?" Speed squinted his eyes at me, and Stroker's eyebrows knitted together. I wasn't in the mood to be rational. I had my own issues with Carly, and now it seemed I was going to let those rule me. Not only was I jonesing over Carly, but I could also say almost positively that when

Speed knew what I wanted from her, he'd feel like he'd need to stand between her and me out of a misguided brotherly duty. He'd learn quickly enough that I would take what he had to dish out if he felt the need, but I also inwardly smiled that Carly wouldn't let him play protector because she had enough in herself to handle things on her own.

"Crusher, I've watched that girl since she arrived as barely an adult. She and Sami never caused any problems around here. I think no matter where she is, she can handle anything she comes up against. She…" Stroker's words were paused as the door flew open and bounced against the wall, causing everyone to look at who dared to bust into the Prez's office.

"What the fu…" was spoken by several and immediately cut off when they saw who it was. Ally walked in like she owned the place, her little hand holding her momma's phone to her ear, eyes taking in everyone in the room as she chattered away to whoever was on the other end of the call. I waited to see how my dad was going to handle this because I'd done the same thing when I was about her age, and it had quickly been taken care of with a stern yelling and me put in my place. But since Ally hadn't lived around club life, it would be interesting to see how it would be handled.

"Ally?" Stroker got her attention though she never missed a beat in talking. "No one is to come in my office without knoc—" he stopped before finishing his sentence, and I'm sure it was because of Ally's action. I know it was the reason I bit the inside of my mouth. Plus, why the others either lowered their heads to hide or covered their mouths to keep from bursting out laughing when Ally's hand that wasn't currently holding the phone raised up and was held palm out in the 'hold on a minute' action as she continued her conversation.

"When you coming to visit me at my daddy's house, Papa? You got to see my bed." Her question at least informed us who she was talking with as she headed toward Sami. "Yep, she's right here. Yep, I've been good. 'K, bye, Papa. Love ya too." Ally handed the phone to Sami as we all listened.

"Hey, Dad? Yeah, did she tell you why? Uh, huh, okay? Sure. Alright. Talk with you later, Dad. Love you too. I will." Sami chuckled at whatever Wild Bill's last comment was and hung up, then looked at Speed while she talked, "Carly is staying at my dad's house. She told him she was staying there a few days and asked if he was cool with that. He thinks she just needs some time to process things."

To say I was happy about her being at the Haven MC would have been a lie. They were still unsure if they'd weeded out everyone affiliated with Stone's attempt to take over.

"I could go to Haven and stay until she is ready to come back." The thought came out of my mouth before I could stop it, and Stroker, Speed, and Sami just stared at me. But leave it to the youngest to question.

"Why?" Ally looked at me with her eyebrows scrunched together, and her question miraculously brought everyone's attention aimed toward me.

49

"Yeah, Crusher, why?" Sami looked up at Speed, her eyebrow raised in question if I had to guess it was because of his tone when he asked the question. When he looked down at her, she shook her head, rolled her eyes, and grabbed Ally's hand.

"Come on, Ally. Let's leave the men so they can have their discussion. We are going to have one of our own about barging into the Prez's office without knocking." Sami turned to Speed. "We're going to the house to finish putting things away. Play nice, it will work out." Speed bent down and kissed Sami, then kissed his daughter's forehead. I watched with the others and wondered if the same thing went through their minds—how Black Hawk was changing.

"I'll see you at the house. And, sweetheart, you roll those eyes at me again, I am going to spank your ass."

"I can show you how to get it a nice shade, Speed." Flirt's words, Speed's head jerked in his direction.

"Don't make me whip your ass in this office." When Speed stepped toward Flirt, Flirt stood. Fuck me, I did not want to break up a fight. The other brothers stood, well, except the dads, who still sat in their chairs shaking their heads.

"Daddy?"

Christ, we forgot the room held a little girl who was watching each of us, but her one word had stopped Speed in his tracks as he faced her.

"What, baby girl?" I watched his face lose every sign of his previous mad when he looked at his daughter.

"Ass is a bad word. Momma said we can't say that." A pin could have been heard hitting the floor. Evidently, it was okay for her to repeat the word while correcting us.

"Okay, baby girl, so noted."

"So, is Momma still going to get a spanking?"

"Not until you go to bed," was said with a cough. I wasn't sure which brother had said it until I saw Preacher smack Devil in the chest.

"Shut up, dic…" Speed caught himself before presumably calling Devil a dickhead and turned back to Ally.

"Can we talk about this after I come home, baby?" Yeah, he was dodging, hoping she'd forget by the time he got there, but Spider didn't forget much from what I'd seen.

"Yep, but if you have to spank Momma, don't make her cry. I don't like when Momma cries." How Ally looked at her dad made me think the last part of her statement was meant as a threat. My lips twitched, and I lifted a brow as I looked at the other brothers, who seemed to be fighting to keep their composure.

Sami looked at Speed, and by the shade of red her face turned, she heard Coast as he tried to whisper under his breath, "She won't cry if he does it right."

Damn, we weren't going to get anything accomplished by the look on Speed's face as he turned in Coast's direction. We would be lucky if the brother send one of us to the hospital.

"See you at the house," Speed said and didn't take his eyes off Coast. Sami turned with Ally toward the door. Nothing was said as we waited for them to leave the office.

As they moved to the door, Ally whispered none too quietly, "Momma, I don't like spankings, do you?" I watched the others' faces, and each held a strained expression, which I was sure my face mimicked.

"Ally, we will talk at home."

"And what's a prezzz's office, Momma? I opened Papa Stroker's door," Ally continued to talk as Sami dragged her through the door. When the latch clicked, the room filled with laughter.

Speed was the first to recover, and he asked, "Now are you going to answer why you would want to travel to Haven, Crusher?"

"Especially since what I've witnessed, you and the deputy can barely be in the same room together without ripping into each other. Russ?" Even in the Prez's office, when I was called by my given name by him, it meant my dad was inquiring, not the president of the club expecting a member to answer. I often wondered how he was able to juggle the two jobs; he'd done them both without ever faltering. A boy couldn't have asked for a better man to be his father. I was the man I was today because of him.

That's why I wouldn't make a rash decision over going after Carly. I knew I couldn't go to Haven's territory, but I could fill the time while waiting for her to return, working out what was going on so we could keep her safe here.

"Let's get down to business and talk out what we know so far, then what we need to find out to obtain the answers. Something more is there. We just need all the pieces," I said, and everyone nodded and started discussing what we did know. I felt Stroker's gaze on me, and when I looked toward him, he smiled and winked.

"You heard the man. Let's get to it," Stroker said, then turned toward the others to join the discussion. It felt good to know the man I admired most in this world seemed to hold complete faith in me. I moved to take a seat with the others, there was nothing but time until Carly came back.

Chapter Four

Carly

The hotel room door closed, and the man wasted no time advancing on me. We'd sat at the bar and had a few drinks, laughing and talking about nothing important. His dark brown hair was cut short, making me think of the military. I'd asked, and he'd told me he'd just gotten out.

"Been back about a month," he said and ran his hand over his hair, "so used to keeping it short, don't know if I'm going to be able to let it grow too long. I'd like it to be long enough for a woman to hold onto while I ride her." He took a drink of his beer, and I stared at him. He turned, smiled, and winked, and I'd known then I was in trouble. He seemed easygoing and talked to me, not at me. When I was talking, I had his full attention—he didn't look around as though he

had someplace better to be. I hadn't dated much because, at first, school was too important to me, and it seemed that every time I accepted a date from one of the guys in my classes, it was assumed we were going to have sex. A few I did sleep with, but others, if I didn't dive into bed with them, they called me the ice bitch.

The job with the sheriff's department came at just the right time, and while going through my initial training, which happened to be with mostly men, I wanted to pass on my merits, not because I slept my way through. So, standing in a hotel room with a man I just met was so not me.

He grabbed my shoulders, pulled me into his chest, bent his head, and took my mouth in a hard kiss that made my knees weak. He bit my bottom lip, and when I gasped, his tongue dove into tangle with mine, and I had the briefest feeling of falling. I'd been kissed, but as his lips moved from mine and traveled down my neck, stopping to nibble on the spot where my shoulder met the end of my neck, those were amateur in comparison, the difference between a young man and a grown one evident. I had so been missing out.

His hands traveled down to my hips, pulling me in closer till I felt the hardness of him pressed against me. I ran my hands down him and untucked his t-shirt to slide my hands under and over his abs. I could tell he was cut as I outlined his six pack with my fingertips. His groan as I ran my fingers over him let me know he was enjoying my touch. When I slipped my hand into the front of his pants, he stepped back, and I felt the loss of his body heat.

"Babe, we got too many clothes on." I watched as his shirt was pulled up and over his head, revealing tan skin and a bare chest with a small amount of golden hair starting at his belly button and out of view into his jeans. Jeans he was unbuttoning and sliding off his hips and *freeing the biggest cock I had ever seen. I licked my lips, and it twitched. "If you don't have clothes out in your truck, you better get out of those before I rip them off you."*

I blinked at his words and looked up into brown eyes full of desire, and for the first time ever, I felt like a desirable woman. I kept my eyes linked with his and started to remove my clothes. When the last piece hit the floor, his eyes broke from mine to run down my body and back up.

"Goddamn, your body is better than I imagined. If you knew all the things I want to do with it, you would grab your clothes and leave." What? Was he joking?

"You want me to leave?" His eyes shot to mine while his hand took hold of his cock and pumped.

"Fuck no. I said you could leave; I didn't say I would let you. Needed in you like yesterday." Before I could respond, I was picked up, and then we were falling. My body hit the bed with him coming down on top of me. He caught himself on his elbows to keep the majority of his weight off me, thank God because though I was of average height, my body was thin with an athletic build. Next to him, I looked dainty and felt more feminine than I had in my whole life.

"What are you waiting for then?" I asked in a voice I didn't recognize as mine. The words came out throaty and laced in need. It was the only encouragement he needed. He lifted up on his knees, reached for the condom I hadn't even seen him set on the bed, and opened and rolled it down his length.

"You might want to lift your hands up to that headboard and hold on. This first time is going to be hard, fast, and explosive." At his words, he stayed on his knees, grabbed my thighs, spread, and pulled me down the bed until my pussy was aligned with his cock. He rested my

legs on his hips, and with his hands free, one hand moved to separate my lips while the other slid his cock through my wetness. "Damn, babe, you are soakin' wet. Hold on," he said and pushed in until he bottomed out, then he stilled, letting me adjust to him. It was sweet, but he promised hard and fast.

"Move, damn it." He grabbed my hips, and that was exactly what he did. He pounded into me, setting a pace that had perspiration breaking out on our skin. I had to do what he told me, and I placed my hands on the headboard to keep him from driving the top of my head against it.

My head bent back, my back arched, and an orgasm racked my body and clenched my walls around his cock. He thrust one more time and followed me as he grunted, and his own body shook as he filled the condom and collapsed down beside me, pulling me to him.

"Christ, hope I have more condoms in my saddlebags, or you are going to be wearing a lot of my cum on your body by the time I get done with you."

My eyes opened to a room filled with sunshine, and I sat up quickly and looked around. Sami's old room. Fucking dream! I threw myself back on the bed and looked over at the clock on the nightstand. Well, shit, it was noon.

It was one when I got out of bed, showered, and dressed. The house was quiet as I went downstairs and headed to the kitchen. I didn't care what time it was, I needed damn coffee. As I went to pass the closed door of Wild Bill's office, I heard muffled voices. I knocked and waited for a reply.

"Enter!" Wild Bill yelled. I swung the door open to find Reed, Hawk, Moose, Pinch, and Crank sitting around the large table in the center of the room.

"I'm going to make some coffee, anyone want any?"

"Sounds good, girlie. Did you sleep okay?" Wild Bill looked me over; it was like he could read my mind as the grin spread across his face. I smiled back.

"Best I've had in a while. Thanks for letting me come here, listening to my whining, and letting me stay at your house. If you don't mind, I want to visit with Macy and Tink today, stay another night and head back to Shades Valley tomorrow."

"You don't have to ask, Carly. You're welcome here anytime, girl. Haven will always be your home. And my house will always be open to you. So no problem. You stay as long as you need to. I'm glad to see the light back in those eyes of yours." Typical of Wild Bill, he got up, walked over, and embraced me. He'd been more of a dad to me than Stone ever had been. I hugged him back. We broke apart, and he took his seat at the head of the table again, and I turned to walk out.

"Hey, since you are part of the family and all, why don't you throw some food together for us while you're in the kitchen?"

"Bite me, Reed," I said and closed the door to the sounds of laughter. Smiling, I headed to the kitchen. Family. It had been a while since I felt like I had one.

Chapter Five

Crusher

After leaving the Prez's office, we walked to the garage that sat behind Speed's house and dove into work on one of the custom jobs. They'd be starting the add-on Monday that would house the parts we currently had stacked in boxes around the main area. When it was done, we'd be able to spread out and work on more than one at a time as we were doing now.

"Hey, did the contractor say how long it would take them to finish that extension?" I sat the oil intake valve on the bench and wiped my hands off.

"Inside a month for total completion if the weather holds good until they get that portion under roof." Speed stood from his spot beside his dad's bike.

"Great, it will be nice to be able to spread out a bit once we get these parts shelved in there," I said just as my phone buzzed. When I pulled it out of my pocket and looked at the screen, there was again 'private caller' showing. I hit the talk button. "Yeah."

"Ummm...is this Russell Davis?" a woman's voice spoke on the other end.

"Who the fuck wants to know?" Finally, a voice but one I'd never heard before.

"It's... never mind," was said, and the caller hung up. The guys stood looking at me.

"First time someone spoke on the other end. I meant to ask you, Coast, to work your magic and see if you could find where these calls are coming from. No number is coming up, just 'private caller' shows on screen. No one ever spoke before when I answered."

"Sure thing, Crusher. If you can go without the phone for a few hours tomorrow, I'll take the chip out of it and see if I can backtrack it. May not be a number showing, but the call is bouncing from somewhere. It could at least give you the area, if not a number. Something or someone might click if when can pinpoint an area where the calls are originating from."

"Thanks, Coast. I should be able to go without the damn thing for a few hours."

"Well, you boys want to go to Soft Tails tonight? Have a few beers, watch a few girls?" Devil hung the tools he'd used.

"I'm in, Devil. How about the rest of you fuckers?" Flirt asked, laying the tarp over the engine parts that were spread out on a drop cloth.

"I'm in, too. Between helping with moving Sami and Spider in, working in here, and sitting with my dad going over all the shit he takes care of for the club, I deserve a drink and to get laid." Jag turned the gas off to the torch he was using. If he hadn't gone to college and then law school, he could have made a decent living as a welder.

"Speed, you in?" I knew Speed had been watching Ally when Sami worked the late shift.

"Sounds good. Sami was off today, but she works tomorrow, so she and Ally will be in bed early. What time do you guys want to go?"

"After dinner. Or do you want to wait until after you put Ally down?" I wasn't going to ask what the twitch to his lips meant. When you weren't getting laid regularly, you could pick out a man who was.

"Nah, we can go after dinner. Best if I don't wait for Ally to go to sleep. I may not want to leave after that." Rags were thrown at Speed from all directions. "What? Can I help it if I got a warm, willing woman that puts up with my shit?"

"Not at all. We just don't want to hear about it," I said, flipped him off, and headed out of the garage. "Text me when you fuckers are ready to roll. I'm going to clean up." I headed in the direction of my house.

"Just the gentlemen I needed to see," Tank said as we walked into Soft Tails. The music was blaring, and the place was full of brothers.

"What's up, man?" I asked and looked around the place.

"Let me get Bull to cover the door for me, and we can talk in Sami's office." We nodded and headed in that direction, knowing Tank would follow after Bull replaced him.

On the way, I stopped by the bar and told Stem to set us up at our usual table with a round. By the time we unlocked the office door and entered, Tank was right behind us and closed the door after he entered.

"It could be nothing, or it could be an issue, but when I closed up, and Bull and I were getting on our rides, we heard bike engines getting closer, so we waited, thinking maybe it was a few of the club members. Instead, three bikes we've never seen went by."

"Not like other riders don't come through, Tank," I said.

"Yeah, but these riders slowed, glanced over, and when they saw Bull and me sitting on our bikes, they sped up. It was dark, so we didn't get a good look. We just know they weren't any of ours."

"Still, that doesn't mean anything. They would have seen the Soft Tails' sign, maybe they slowed to see if it was still open," Speed said, and Tank shook his head.

"Why don't you think that is it, Tank?" I would blow this shit off any other time, but with the crap over Carly, I didn't want to take any chances.

"Go ask Roscoe. I overheard him talking about three riders to the group at his table, but I hadn't gotten a chance to ask him about them tonight. I got a gut feeling they could be the same fellows." Yeah, my gut was agreeing with Tank.

"Where did he see them?" Speed asked.

"Not sure didn't hear that part."

"We'll check with him. Thanks, Tank." He nodded at me, and I headed to the door as Flirt opened it.

"Speed, Spider's birthday is coming up next month. I and some of the guys wondered if you and Sami minded if we brought some stuff by your house for her?" I chuckled at Tank's question while we all walked out of the office. We waited while Speed closed and locked the door.

"Sami plans to have a party for her," Speed answered

"That is why we wanted to drop her present off ahead of time. We didn't want to show up and scare any of the kids there." Tank looked at Speed and frowned like Speed had missed the reason for the drop-off.

"Not a kid birthday party, man. A club birthday party for her. Everyone will be invited. Figure we can have a cookout in the yard behind the club since everything is out there. My place can't hold everyone." As I listened to the exchange, I looked around and spotted Roscoe and turned in his direction, Speed followed while the others headed to our table where Layne was setting down our drink order.

"That is great. I will let the other guys know," Tank said and headed back to his spot at the door.

"What's so funny?" Speed glared at me when I chuckled and stopped at the table Roscoe was sitting at.

"Man, you do realize that little girl has managed to do what grown men haven't?" When he didn't answer, I continued. "You know, brought a whole MC down to bow in front of her. I think if you told them she wanted a dress-up party with Disney characters, they would do it. And, brother, that would be some funny shit to see." I laughed.

"No shit, you may have to defend your seat as president when she gets older because the guys might follow her if she asked them to," Speed said, drawing the stares from the men at the table.

"Damn straight, the girl is going to be hell on wheels when she gets grown, and, Speed, you are going to need to keep a loaded shotgun to keep motherfuckers from chasing after her," Roscoe said, then laughed.

Speed looked at him and sneered, "Nah, I'm going to have her so tough; she will be able to kick their asses herself. No man's going to run over my baby girl."

I looked over at him and cocked my eyebrow. "Uh, didn't you steamroll over Sami to get what you wanted?" All the men at the table laughed with me.

"Shut up, asshole. Aren't you supposed to be checking with Roscoe and not busting my balls?"

I shook my head at his attempt to deflect before I looked down at Roscoe. "Yeah, Roscoe, Tank mentioned you saw a few unknown riders come through town?"

"Not through town. I uh...was coming out of Sue's place as three riders passed by her house. I never seen them before, so I got on my bike and followed in the direction they went. Never caught up to them, though. Don't know why they would be on that street unless they made a wrong turn coming through town."

"Not sure either. But if you see them again, give me a call." I looked at Speed, and his eyes met mine.

Yeah, we hadn't had a problem with unknown riders hanging around in our parts, so why now?

I glanced back at Roscoe. "Thanks, man," I turned to head to our table and said over my shoulder, "Don't think we missed the part about you coming out of Sue's place. We'll save that info for later." Speed and the others laughed. However, Roscoe was never to be outdone.

"You boys are just jealous because I get more action than you do. Speed should be glad I didn't steal Sami before he came back."

"Ah, Roscoe, you couldn't handle my woman."

"Nobody likes a bragger, son."

Speed and I laughed all the way to our table. After sitting down, we told the others about the riders Roscoe had seen.

"Are you thinking the same as me? Stone and a couple of his flunkies?" Coast asked, and I nodded in agreement.

"Sonofabitch, what is he hanging around close to here for. Sami told me he hasn't been in contact with Carly since the shit exploded at Haven. I'm not sure if it even has to do with her. Thinking it's Black Hawk he is interested in. At least if you try to interpret the note he sent Cutter." Speed and the rest of us seemed to be on the same page.

"It could be Ally, Speed. She has a tie with both clubs. Asshole might think with her, he could call the shots where we are all concerned." The fire that flashed in Speed's eyes would make the strongest of men fear for their lives.

"Crusher's right, brother. He is a lowlife, and nothing is more dangerous than a lowlife with nothing to lose," Flirt said.

"I disagree. Nothing is more dangerous than a club that would do anything to protect what is theirs," Devil said.

"Fuckin' A, brother. He can't hurt either club if his ass is six feet under." I would have smiled if the shit wasn't so serious, and I wasn't more worried about Carly than I was before. If her dad was around, for whatever reason, I could guarantee it wasn't good. Speed's cell rang, stopping our conversation. While he talked, I looked toward the stage where Lindy's routine started. The girl could move and bend in all directions, I knew, because I'd had her in most of them. But as I watched her drop her top to the floor and spin around the pole, her tits jiggling with her movements, I didn't have any reaction. Damn, the blonde in my thoughts was going to be the death of me, and wasn't it funny that the thought of her did bring a reaction as my jeans tightened under the strain of the erection.

"Crusher, you listening?" Speed's voice drew me out of my thoughts.

"Yeah."

"Carly called Sami and told her she would be back tomorrow. She visited with a couple of the ol' ladies today at the Haven clubhouse. She told Sami she would talk with her when she got back," Speed finished.

"That's not safe, brother, and you know it. Especially with the shit about riders around here. I'm telling you, it is that fucker. Give me Wild Bill's number, I'm going to call and talk to him about this shit. The fucker is Haven's man, so I don't see an issue discussing it." Speed scrolled through his contacts until he found Wild Bill's number. I programmed it in and heard it dialing. "Thanks, man."

When Wild Bill answered, I laid everything out for him, and he agreed. He and a few of his men would ride with her, and we would meet them at a halfway mark to ride the rest of the way back to Black Hawk. I hung up and told the brothers what we had planned.

"Everyone onboard for the road trip tomorrow?" I asked.

"Hell yeah," Speed was the first to answer.

"You sure you want to make that trip? What if he is in town, waiting for us to give him an opening to grab Spider?" Speed's face turned bright red at my words.

"I will kill him with my bare fucking hands if he tries, but my place as an enforcer is to protect you. I have to trust the club to protect my family when I'm not able to be there. We can contact some of the guys to hang out at the clubhouse and around the houses tomorrow. I don't want to scare Ally or Sami, but she won't be going to work tomorrow, so that will cut down on splitting the club to watch the both of them. I'll handle it when I get home."

"Trust you to set it up, brother."

"I'm in for the road trip, and Brax could stay close to your house, Speed. No one would get near Sami and Ally with him around," Flirt said.

"What's his deal? I see him at Soft Tails sometimes. As far as I can tell, he's doing a great job as a prospect. But he doesn't talk much, and I don't see him take up with any of the women that come on to him," Speed asked Flirt. The dude had come to Black Hawk with Flirt when he transitioned out of the service. I was curious myself as to the reason.

"We were coming back from a mission. We stepped off the transport plane, and the Colonel met us. He walked straight to Brax because he was one of the few men who had family that would meet us when we were allowed to tell them we were headed home. Brax's wife was one of them. She'd come and bring their little boy. That day, instead, the Colonel informed him they had been killed by a drunk driver the night before. They were hit head-on when the dumbass crossed the median to their side. The Colonel had told him they didn't suffer; they didn't even know what hit them it had happened so fast, the witnesses said. He went quiet after that, then he got out at the same time as me. With no other family, he did not really know what he was going to do. I asked if he rode, and he said not in a few years. He sold his bike when his kid was born, it scared his wife. I told him about the club, and he bought his bike the next day, and then we headed here."

Damn was said at the same time by all of us. "He's a big bastard. How the hell was he a SEAL?" I asked.

Flirt laughed, "Don't let his size fool you. He can move just as stealthily as a man half his size. And you are just going to have to trust me when I say he is one of the deadliest men I've known."

"Why is he still a prospect?" Devil asked.

"Prez said he needed to do his time like everyone else. As we did," Flirt answered.

"I'll have Prez put him on Sami and Ally tomorrow while we are gone. He can be extra protection." Speed nodded to me, and so did Flirt. "We should be ready then."

"Fuck yeah, my ass is ready for a nice ride with you guys. We haven't done that since we've all gotten back," Jag said.

"Then tomorrow it is. Road trip," I said.

"You think you should call Stroker, run this shit past him before we get ahead of ourselves?" Jag asked.

"You're going to be my VP one day. Are you going to question everything I do then, too?" I asked. It was wrong, I knew it, but the thought of Carly riding all the way back by herself didn't sit right with me. Not under the circumstances.

"Asshole, that isn't it. I don't want the dads to think we are already pushing them out." Jag stared me down.

Yeah, and the funny part, he was doing the VP jobs. There had to be loyalty between the members in leadership positions in a club, but if the club functioned right—it wasn't blind loyalty.

"I know. I'll go see him after I speak with Wild Bill and set time and meeting place. You guys ready to head out?" I rose when everyone nodded in agreement. On our way out, I laid cash on the bar to cover our tab and Layne's tip. We walked out, mounted our bikes, and headed back to Black Hawk.

As we drove in, Brax was at the gate, and Flirt and Speed stopped to talk with him as the rest of us continued to the clubhouse. Sitting on the porch of the clubhouse as we pulled up were Dare, Shakes, Daisy, and the dads.

"You boys are back early. Soft Tails not busy tonight?" Stroker yelled from his spot.

"Nah, but I have a few things to talk over with you." I walked up on the porch, and Stroker stood.

"Club business?" Stroker asked as he walked toward the door.

"Yeah, Prez."

"Everyone needed for this talk?" He asked and cocked his brow.

"Yes." I looked over to the other men who were already starting to stand.

"Okay, come on, let's go to my office." Stroker headed in just as Speed and Flirt pulled up.

"Dare, you might want to come in and hear this, too," I mentioned, and Dare stood and followed us all in. When everyone was seated, I started to tell them about the riders that had been seen and the ride we were taking tomorrow to intercept Carly.

"Okay, sounds like you have it all planned out. We will be around to handle anything here. Is that all you needed?" Stroker asked.

"Yes, we are headed out in the morning. I'll text you when we are heading back." I looked at my dad, and for the first time, I didn't recognize the look on his face.

"Alright, you boys have a good night. I want to talk some things over with my officers." The man was all Prez at that point, and we stood to leave along with Dare while Speed, who was now one of the leaders, stayed. "Dare, you can stay for this. Speed, you won't be needed for this one."

Speed stood from his chair as Dare sat back, and then the six of us walked out of the office and to our bikes before anyone said anything.

"What the fuck just happened in there? I've been in on their little meetings since they threw the enforcer patch at me." Speed looked back to the clubhouse. Shakes and Daisy had evidently decided not to hang around and wait, the porch was empty when we walked out.

"Do you think they are pissed we decided to do it before informing them?" Coast asked.

"Nah, I don't think that would be it. When have you known my dad to hold in anything if it bothered him or your dads for that matter? They'll let us know if we need to know." Heads nodded, and we mounted our bikes and headed to our homes. I hoped once there, I would be able to get some sleep, any sleep because I had a feeling that tomorrow I needed to be rested.

Chapter Six

Carly

This was all fucking bullshit. *The little woman needs a damn escort.* I got to Haven on my own, not like I couldn't find my way back to Shades Valley. Men!

I got up and packed my saddlebags, then went to sit down with a cup of coffee just as the front door opened, and in walked Reed, Moose, and Crank. I said good morning as they grunted and reached for the coffee pot.

"Late night, boys?"

"How can you be chipper? You drank with us," Reed griped and took a big gulp of coffee.

"Probably because she went to bed while you dumbasses had me drop you off at the clubhouse. Who did you get to drop you off since your bikes were left here?" Wild Bill asked as he walked into the kitchen.

"Hawk, now we owe him. His ass will wait until he needs some shit work done, and then he will call the favor it in." Moose flopped in the chair beside me. "Sugar, you sure you gotta go back today." I laughed, and he grabbed his head.

"Yes, I have a few things I need to deal with."

He nodded and then closed his eyes as he took a drink of his coffee before he replied, "Fine, it won't take long for the fresh air to clear my head."

That was when I clued into why they were at Wild Bill's so early, it wasn't just to pick up their bikes.

Wild Bill frowned at Moose and then informed me that he and the others were only riding halfway with me. Which wasn't so bad until he added that the Black Hawk MC men would meet us at the halfway point and ride the rest of the way in with me. I may or may not have called them every name in the book.

"You done?" Wild Bill asked, and I glared back at him. "We're still going with you, so everyone get their shit together, and let's hit the road. I don't want to be late to the meetup spot."

Riding down the road in the middle of the four men as if I was a piece of china that would break if a bug hit me was irritating. Hell, they were riding tucked so close that I had to look up at the sky just to make sure we were actually outside riding.

Yes, I may be exaggerating some, but if a vehicle got too close to me, they moved in closer. Not that I thought bitching would make them stop. I know they never would, but I couldn't let them have their way too easily.

Reed signaled to the sign on the right side of the road as we passed it. Presumably, it was our exit because he flicked his blinker on right before we reached the turn.

We pulled right up to the pumps at Leonard's Gas and Go. When we pulled in, I saw the six bikers sitting off to the side. As we stopped, they headed toward us. I placed the pump in my tank and, out of the corner of my eye, watched Crusher as his long legs ate up the ground like he was on a mission, with Speed not far behind him.

Great, the gang was all here.

Speed greeted the Haven men and came to stand before me. He pulled the sunglasses off, and when those intense blue eyes focused on me in that second, I understood why Sami folded so easily around him. His square jaw, high cheekbones, and face framed with black hair were an intimidating picture. His lips were perched and, combined with his stare, made me wonder what he saw and thought. Everything around us went quiet, the only sound was the clicking of the pumps as the tanks filled. Then the breath was knocked out of me, and I found my face buried in a huge chest and encased in two huge arms.

"Don't ever run without talking to me. I understand it was a shock. I had the same reaction, but damn, does it really matter how we found out. You and I share blood, and we have fucking lost enough time because our mother chose not to tell us. That shit is on her, and I don't plan to waste any more on why she would do it, and neither should you. We're going to get to know each other with no regrets about time lost. Understand?" Speed said, then stepped back, releasing me.

I looked up at him, his expression the same as before, until he smiled at me. "I see now why Sami can't say no to you."

Speed's expression changed to a smirk. "You'll get used to it. We're family, and it doesn't matter how we got to be, we just are. You'll figure out soon enough that if I want it, I usually get it, little sis," he said with not an ounce of shame in his voice.

"Really, little sis? I just find out we are related, and you decide to start our relationship out by insulting my size?" I cocked my eyebrow at him.

"Did we not just cover that I get my way?" he said, and his grin grew bigger.

"You know we will be screwed in a few years, right?" I watched his eyebrows draw together at my words.

"What makes you think that?" he asked.

"Ally already shares your looks. If she gains your attitude—no one will be safe." I couldn't help it; I laughed.

"Fuck, when were we safe before?" Reed said, and the silence of the moment was broken. Well, until Crusher moved in behind me.

"Taking off by yourself was an asinine move. With the shit that went on at Haven, your ass should have known better." I could physically feel his eyes burning into my back.

I hung the pump back in its slot and capped my tank before I turned to face him. When I did, I damn near smacked right into his chest, he was so close. A do-rag covered his head with a small amount of brown hair curled up over the edge, and his eyes were hidden by his sunglasses. He crossed his arms over his chest and looked down at me. I made several decisions while at Haven, and his acting like a dick made me reevaluate one.

What the hell, every time this man opened his mouth, it brought the worst out of me, whether he was right or not. This time was no different, so as if I had no control over myself, I jabbed my finger in his chest, "Do you think because I have blonde hair that I'm clueless? That I don't know what went on at Haven. Are you assuming that I can't take care of myself? I missed the memo where you get to tell me what the fuck to do. So why don't you go fuc..." Before I could finish, I was shoved to the ground, then popping sounds filled the air, tires squealed, and I felt a white-hot burning in my thigh. The commotion around me picked up, bikes were started, and the smell of burning rubber laced the air, and I could only listen. Though I had words in my mind, I couldn't push them out of my mouth, the pain was excruciating. I could literally feel my blood pumping through my body.

"Carly! And get away from the fucking gas pumps," was screamed from somewhere close, and then a pair of arms grabbed me up, and I felt the person running while whispering to me, "Hang on, baby, I got you. I got you." Then more loudly, "Devil, I need you here, brother!"

Crusher, it was Crusher who held me, whispered to me as I shivered.

My last thought before blackness took me was when had it turned cold?

Chapter Seven

Crusher

"What the fuck is taking so long?" I asked the nurse behind the desk. I wished we would have been at home at our hospital, but there'd been no time. Carly had been transported to the closest hospital from the gas station.

I'd never been so scared in my life. Not when I was in the desert and bullets flew by me and my unit. Not when I was alone and laid on a roof surrounded by the enemy while I waited for my target to step out from their cover so I could take the kill shot. I'd done and seen a lot in my time in the military, but watching the blood pump out of Carly's thigh at an alarming rate made every other incident I was involved in seem insignificant.

One minute we had been standing there as a group, talking, joking, and then the pickup moving a little too slow on the road caught our attention, and when the window went down on the passenger side, I knew it wasn't just someone wanting to feel the wind blowing in. Everything happened in seconds, the first bullet fired from the gun sticking out of the window hit the pole separating the pumps. I knocked Carly to the ground but heard two more pops, then someone yelled about getting away from the pumps. I grabbed her up and started to move before the sound of return fire entered the mix, shortly followed by the squealing of tires. When I raised up, I had made it to our bikes that had been parked to the side, and I looked around to see Speed, Coast, Reed, and the man they called Moose all had weapons out. I looked down at the woman I held, and Carly's eyes were closed. As I ran my eyes over her body, they stopped on her right thigh, and the blood was soaking through her jeans at an alarming rate. I yelled for Devil, and he raised from his squatted position and headed my way.

When we talked about making this trip, I first thought that not everyone needed to come. However, Devil being there had been the one thing the paramedics said that had kept Carly from bleeding out there in the parking lot. Lance Cummings, Devil, had spent his army career as a 68W, his training as a medic had saved countless lives, and today he could add one more to his tally. He'd acted swiftly and proficiently in tying off Carly's thigh with a makeshift tourniquet to stop the bleeding.

Coast, Flirt, Reed, and Crank pulled out of the parking lot after the fuckers while Speed and I were torn between Carly and wanting to go on the hunt but only for a minute. The others would find them if we were lucky, and family meant more at the time than vengeance. That could always be done later.

"Sir, like the last time you asked. They will come out and inform the family after they evaluate Ms. Monroe. Are you related to the victim?" She looked up from her computer screen at me.

"I'm her brother," Speed said as he walked up beside me. "She was unconscious when they brought her in, can you at least tell me if she woke up for them?"

"No, sir. They are evaluating her in the back, they will let you know when they are done. I'm sorry." The nurse turned back to her computer as if to dismiss us.

"This is bullshit." I paced back to the seating area where Wild Bill, Jag, Moose, and Devil sat, dealing with the local cops.

"Mr. Borelli, our town here is relatively quiet. Though you have been more than cooperative, I doubt this is a random drive-by." The officer said to Wild Bill, then looked at each of us, then continued, "By the vest, you gentlemen—"

"Cuts, they're called cuts, Officer Comer. And though we appreciate your dedication to your job, your assumptions we can do without. We told you what happened. You got to ask your questions, and we answered those. We even supplied you with conceal and carry licenses for our weapons. We went as far as to explain we met at the gas station, so Ms. Monroe didn't have to ride the roads alone from visiting her hometown. Considering she was randomly attacked at one of your so-called quiet town gas stations, we are glad her brother asked us to come on the trip. So unless you have more questions, I think you have all you need. Maybe you and your partner could hunt down the shooters since they are running loose while we are here and will continue to be here until Ms. Monroe is released." Damn, I'd never seen Jag in attorney mode. It was fucking impressive. Officer Comer was determined to get the last word.

"You didn't explain where the other four of your ga...crew went? Why are they not here?" Yeah, we all caught that he wanted to call us a gang, and his sneer made him a bigger dick than I thought.

"They went to pick up some clothing for these two," he pointed to me and Devil, who wore Carly's blood on our clothing, "members, Officer Comer. Just members, not gang members, nor part of a crew. We are members of an MC. It stands for Motorcycle Club, officer, in case you don't understand the term." Wild Bill was even impressed with Jag, if the smirk on his face was an indication.

"It took four to purchase clothing?" the officer asked snidely.

"Considering we were shot at a gas station in this town, a couple more of us should have gone with them." Later I would recall this and laugh at the look on the officer's face, but now I just wanted answers on Carly.

"Hope Ms. Monroe recovers quickly. We'll leave you men for now. And I will be sure to call the sheriff's station in each of your counties to check on those licenses you provided." The officer and his partner stood.

"Go ahead and give the sheriffs calls. They've both been notified that you would be calling. They have your name, shouldn't be too hard to get a hold of them. Oh, did we not inform you that Ms. Monroe was one of our sheriff's deputies? That must have slipped my mind. Have a good day, officers."

We all watched as Officer Comer and his partner stopped at the nurse's desk and said something before walking out.

"Goddamn, son, we could use you at Haven. Nothing like pissing off the cops and being correct in doing so," Wild Bill said and shook his head.

"No offense, I'll stick with Black Hawk. I like my relaxation time, and I don't think I would get much at Haven."

Wild Bill slapped Jag on the back, "You are probably right."

The doors swung open from the back, and a man in a white coat walked toward us. "Who is Ms. Monroe's family?" The doctor clarified more when we all answered. "Her *immediate* family?"

"That would be me. Kane Weston." Speed elaborated at the doctor's questioning look, "I'm her half-brother, same mother, different dads." The doctor nodded.

"Well, do you know your blood type, Mr. Weston? Ms. Monroe has lost a lot. She is currently being prepped for surgery to repair the artery, and with her blood type, we only have a couple of pints in our bank, it may not be necessary, but we could use a little extra in case she needs it. She's type A-."

"Not a problem, doc. I have the same blood type, A-. Where do you need me?" A nurse walked out from the back while the doctor was talking to us.

"Just follow the nurse. She'll take you back to donate."

"Doc, how is she doing? Is she going to be okay?" I needed validation on her being okay, and thank God Speed waited to follow the nurse because I didn't think they would talk with me otherwise.

"We aren't expecting any issues to occur, but since we can't know what will happen when someone is put under, we take all precautions. Barring nothing going wrong, she should come through just fine. Depending on her progress after surgery will dictate how long she has to stay in the hospital. We will let Mr. Weston know how everything goes after the surgery. Now I need to get up there, they probably have her prepped. Mr. Weston, if you will follow the nurse, we will be set. Gentlemen." The doctor turned and went back through the swinging doors with Speed and the nurse following.

Devil stood, pulled his cell out, and walked toward the outside doors. "Something wrong, brother?" I asked.

"Going to call my dad. I need him to check something for me. I'll let you know, it might not be anything, but I'm just curious." He walked out before I could question him further.

I sat down beside Wild Bill, and he looked over at me, "What's up with you and Carly?"

Jag coughed, stood, and walked to the vending machines while I faced Wild Bill. Moose stood, looked at Wild Bill, and stated, "Prez, if before the gunfire erupted was anything indication, I'd be more apt to ask when the wedding is and if you needed to bring a shotgun for it." Moose walked to the vending machines to join Jag.

"Who needs a shotgun?" Speed asked as he sat down, pulling off the cotton ball from his arm and looking at it. He must not have seen any fresh blood on it because he stood, threw the cottonball and tape in the trash, and returned to his seat."

"Maybe me. I asked your friend here what's between Carly and him. You, I'll get to in a minute. Get ready to answer some questions about when you are marrying my daughter."

The saying 'saved by the bell' came to mind as Crank and Flirt walked into the waiting area. When my eyes met Flirt's, he nodded, which answered why Coast and Reed hadn't followed them in. They'd caught up with the occupants of the truck.

Chapter Eight

Crusher

After informing the nurse at the desk, we stepped outside with Flirt and Crank and found a sitting area off to the side. When we reached it, I noticed Devil first, and he looked up from where he was sitting and quickly ended his call to walk over and join us.

"Where are they at?" Wild Bill was the first to speak.

"Keg called Hawk. He is sending Shock and Freak to pick them up, Prez," Crank answered. I wouldn't have known who Crank was referring to if Reed hadn't introduced himself by his club name. Sami and Carly never called him by it.

"Why are your boys coming down to get them? Black Hawk might want to deal with them. Don't forget, we were there too." I looked at Wild Bill.

"The important reason they shot Carly. Do you want more? If Keg called back for transportation, they're from Haven, which means I got a couple more of Stone's little following hanging around, buying their time, spying for that weasel. Crank, who the fuck was it?"

"Tater and his brother, Spud." This was not the time or place, but I had to ask.

"Are those serious names?" Wild Bill shook his head.

"They got the names because they have to have potatoes at every meal, doesn't matter: breakfast, lunch, supper, they eat them. Spud was stripped of his patch right before I took over after my dad's death. Dad nailed him for siphoning off the top on runs. Spud paid back what Pops calculated he took, that and the fact Tater was Stone's buddy, and Stone vouched for Tater. They didn't kill the fucker. Stone had moved up quickly in the club. His first leadership position in Haven was as an enforcer. When the VP died, Stone was voted in.

"I stripped Tater of his patch after Stone went on the run. So they are going back to Haven because I need some info from them. After that, if there is anything left, be glad to give you a call."

"Where do they have them at? Going to be a couple of hours before your boys get here?" I looked at Flirt.

"Abandoned farmhouse, the edge of town, you can't see it from the road. The only reason we knew that is where they went was the dust cloud from the dirt road they were flying on. We parked our bikes where they couldn't be seen from the road and walked through the field to get to the house. They weren't staying there, we checked. Plus, Coast got them to admit they had seen the road and just took it to get off the main one. They didn't know the house was there either till they pulled up." If Haven left the guys with Coast a little longer, I had no doubt the man could get the info out of them. When he left Delta Force, the CIA had recruited him heavily for SOG, Special Operations Group. But Emery Cortez had been ready to come home like the rest of us.

"They coming here after Haven picks those two up, Flirt?" While I waited for Flirt to answer, I noticed Devil had Wild Bill off to the side talking with him. I knew Devil was on to something, and he would let us know when he was ready. My phone rang, and I pulled it out. When I looked down at the screen, private caller was there again. Fuck, I had forgotten, with everything going on, that Coast was supposed to track that shit today. I wasn't in the mood to worry about that shit; Carly was my priority now. I was ready to admit that she became my priority the day I met her. Crazy? Fuck yeah. However, I'd been all over the world with the military and slept with every type of woman, but none radiated or showed the kind of strength Carly had.

My phone rang again, as did Speed's. What the fuck was going on today? Saying shit seemed to hit the fan was an understatement. Devil was still standing by Wild Bill, who was currently on the phone, Flirt stood with Crank and

Moose talking, and Jag was standing between Speed and me as we answered our phones.

As I listened to Stroker talk to me, Speed's 'goddammit' alerted me to the fact he was talking to Sami, and it was said loud enough to draw the other men's attention too.

"Yeah. Everyone's okay, though? Good. Yeah, we got it all handled on this end. Sure thing, Prez, I'll let them know." I hung up just as Speed was finishing his call.

"You first, Speed," I said.

"It was probably the same info you were getting from the Prez, except mine was laced with being scared but moving toward the pissed-off woman." Speed took a deep breath, and I knew he was trying to calm himself down.

"Don't tell me that son-of-a-bitch made a play for my daughter and granddaughter? I will peel that asshole's skin off his body one layer at a time when I get a hold of him. He should have stayed gone. Now that I know he is back, I will lift every rock until I find him." Wild Bill's face made me fear he was going to be headed for the bed beside Carly.

Speed looked at Wild Bill, "Only if you get that bastard first. He has upset my woman and my daughter, his days are numbered. He should have kept his ass away from Black Hawk, now, he is stuck in the middle of two clubs, and his only option is death because even the choice of how he dies is taken away. It will be slow, it will be painful, and then his life will be over.

"Sami sounded more pissed than scared. Seems Stone didn't come himself. ID on the one Brax nailed was Toby

Sams. Sami let Sheriff Lance know he went by the club name Creeper. Sheriff Lance came out, asked some questions, and talked with Brax. The coroner already came and picked up the body. No charges were made on Brax. They had to have been watching because when Brax stopped the guy at the gate, he told Brax he was sent out to get some last minute measures on the garage extension. Brax stepped into the shack and texted Stroker because he noticed the biker boots the guy had on when he went to the window of the truck. Sami said since he never got to the clubhouse, Ally had no clue what was going down. The dads had been playing games with her when Brax had texted. The dads told Sami they would be back and that they needed to check on something. Sami understood they were trying to evade saying anything in front of Ally. They wouldn't let her even go down to the gate after it was over." Speed shook his head and then finished, "I think that is why she is mad. You know from Prez what went down at the gate, so what was it?"

"They got on their bikes and rode down the drive as if they were heading out for a ride. He figures they have been slithering around the area because the guy made them when they got closer to the gate. Prez pulled his gun out when the guy turned to aim his at Brax in the shack. He wasn't there, so he turned the other way, and Brax stepped up to the window and shot Creeper in the eye. He blew off the back of his skull, which is why they wouldn't let her physically ID him. They only showed her his license.

"They called Sheriff Lance then. When he left, he told Stroker that he would have his deputies go around to any abandoned places they knew of and check them out. He figures they have to be staying somewhere out of the way so they wouldn't draw attention. Stroker said to tell everyone nice job and to stay safe. He wants updates on Carly as soon as we get any info." As if someone was listening, the nurse stepped out of the doors and was looking around. Jag spotted her and pointed. Speed hurried over to her as the rest of us followed.

"Mr. Weston, your sister is out of surgery and in recovery. The doctor said he would be down in just a few minutes to speak with you."

"Thank you, ma'am." The nurse turned and went back through the doors. We all stood there for a minute, letting everything that had happened this day sink in. Carly was in recovery, and Sami and Ally were safe. I took one more deep breath and walked back into the hospital.

No sooner than we entered the family waiting area, the doctor came in and walked over to Speed as I stood beside him. "Your sister did great. I had to go deep into her thigh to get to the bullet. You know, of course, it had nicked her femoral artery, I repaired it, but since it is the main artery in the thigh, she will have to take it easy for several weeks. This is essential since the artery is weakened. We don't want to put any additional strain on it. The bullet was lodged in the muscle, it took a little time to get out. I didn't want to do more damage to the muscle than was already done. So what all this boils down to is she will be in some extreme pain while the muscle and the surrounding area heal. Her outer sutures will have to be removed in two weeks, but that can be done at your local hospital. I'm going to recommend therapy to strengthen the muscle back after it heals. That, too, can be done in her hometown. But that will be after the artery heals too. I'm going to keep her for at least three days. If she does well, I will possibly release her, if she isn't doing well, then she is looking to be with us for a minimum of a week. I'll know more after she wakes. Do you have any questions, Mr. Weston?" I didn't give Speed the chance to ask.

"When can we see her?"

"After she comes out of recovery. I will let the nurses know to inform you when she is moved to a room. Have someone page me if you need me to answer any more questions you might think of later." The doctor shook our hands and left.

"Thank fuck." Speed ran his hand down his face. The day had been hard, but maybe a little more for him. "I thought five years ago that the loss of my dad was hard. If today would have gone another way, I don't think I would have been able to come back from the loss. I can't even fathom what it would be like, brother."

"You don't need to. Everyone is safe. Carly is banged up a little, but she will bounce back. We help Haven nail down the fuckwad, and it is clear sailing."

"You're right, Crusher. Just needed to get it out of my system. We might as well sit down and wait for Carly to wake." Everyone took seats to wait. Wait for Carly to wake up, wait for Haven's men to get there for the pickup. I should thank the military for my patience. Though they were

95

running thin, I at least wasn't jumping out of my skin. I'd forgotten about Devil and what he had been checking on until he spoke.

"This has been a shit day, but I'm going to add to it. If I'm wrong, I will own it. However, I don't think I am." He paused, and all eyes went to him.

"You went out to call your dad after Speed was asked to give blood. Whatever you got working in your head, share it." Devil nodded to me, then focused on Speed.

"When the doctor said Carly's blood type was A- and you had the same Speed, it hit me as odd because A- is kinda rare. Approximately six percent of the world has it."

"That means what, Devil? You are losing me," Speed frowned, and I had to admit I was not following either. The only one who seemed to know where Devil was headed was Wild Bill.

"To have any negative Rh factor in your blood, it takes both parents to carry the negative Rh because if either carries the positive Rh, it most always overrides the negative. The A type blood is common, except for if both parents are O type, the children will only be O, no other type will come through." Devil spoke as if we all had medical training.

"Christ, Devil, who cares. What the hell are you saying?" My brain was on overload.

"In a nutshell. Carly isn't Speed's half-sister; she is his full-blooded sister." I turned to Speed when Devil finished, and he still wore the frown, but his eyes could've frozen an open flame.

"That damn bitch left Black Hawk pregnant? Fuck me, she just keeps reaching out of the grave to spread her shit. Are you sure, Devil?" Speed asked.

"I'm not going to say I'm one hundred percent, but a swab of your and Carly's mouths is all that is needed. When I called Dad, I had him check the records for your dad's type, he was A- too. Wild Bill got Stone's and Clarice's blood types. Stone was O+, Clarice O-, we know she gave birth to Carly, but no way Stone is her dad. I'm not saying I'm right about Cutter, Speed, but fuck, man. That is one big coincidence if he's not."

My friend turned and punched the wall. "Think I should know for sure before we tell Carly? Damn it, I'm pissed," he slapped the wall.

"Are you mad at Carly, Speed? Do you think seeing it on paper is going to change the results?" Wild Bill asked, standing.

Speed turned around and looked at him, "Fuck no. I have no doubt she is my sister. I'm pissed about all we missed. My dad was a hard man, and he never asked anyone to do something he wouldn't do himself, but he expected when he asked for something that it was done to the best of your ability because that is how he lived life. From the military to becoming a part of Black Hawk, to being a dad, and to know he missed out where Carly is concerned pisses me off for him, while it has me sorry for the loss that Carly wasn't afforded the same opportunity I was. Cutter would have done the same for her. They both missed out because one selfish fucking woman didn't get her way." Speed shook his head, his face carrying a look of disgust.

"The test takes a few days, Speed. Are you sure you want to wait for the results before you talk to Carly?" Wild Bill held us his hand to stop my brother from talking before he finished, "Carly has always been strong her entire life, son. That girl never let the way Stone and Clarice acted keep her down or mold her in any way. I think their behavior only made her work harder, not to be seen as weak as they were. Stone was and is a drunk, and Clarice, well, she stayed tweaked. Carly isn't going to take kindly to being kept in the dark until you see fit to share. Because, Speed, there may not be a physical resemblance to you two, but goddamn if you both don't have the same 'go after what you want' personality." Wild Bill chuckled.

"No shit! That answers a lot, doesn't it, Prez?" Keg's voice had us all turning around. He and Coast had entered the room and evidently unnoticed for a bit if they heard what was just discussed. Coast walked over with a bag and handed it to me.

"We stopped on our way here. Heard you and Devil could use a change of clothes." I slapped Coast on the shoulder in a thank you gesture.

"Taking everything went smooth on the transfer?" I asked.

"Done," was the only word Coast said before he went over to Flirt and Jag and sat down with them.

"Prez, you think Carly is going to want to come back to Haven and recuperate?" Keg asked Wild Bill, drawing my and Speed's attention as they talked. Speed beat me in answering.

"She will go to Black Hawk."

"She was raised at Haven. If she wants to come there, we will welcome her as we always have." Wild Bill glared back at Speed. I wouldn't let her go to Haven if it was the last thing I did, but I wasn't ready to share that information. Besides, I knew Speed well enough to know he wasn't going to let that happen.

"Carly may have been raised as part of Haven, but she is Black Hawk. So there is no confusion; she will be recuperating there."

"You think you are going to get her to stay at Black Hawk?" Keg said, and Moose laughed, and Wild Bill just smiled.

"It will be easy enough. If I can't get her to cooperate, Crusher will," Speed's words had me turning toward him.

"What makes you think she will listen to me?" Wild Bill's laughter at my words pissed me off.

"Please, now is not the time to act like there is nothing going on between you or had gone on between you; take your pick. But give us credit for not being stupid, brother. Do you forget I know you? You all act like I'm the only one who goes after what they want. It offends me." The rest of our friends laughed at Speed's statement. They and I both knew it took a lot to offend our friend.

"You telling me that you aren't going to give me shit for going after your sister?" I didn't have to wait long for Speed to answer me.

"Why the hell would I be upset that one of the best men I know wants to be involved with my sister? Damn, Crusher." He shook his head as if he couldn't believe my thinking. And I wondered if I wasn't giving my friend and brother enough credit. At least until he continued. "Now, if you hurt her, that will be another matter." I couldn't hold my grin back.

"Excuse me." The lady's voice had us facing the door. "The doctor said to inform you, gentlemen, that Ms. Monroe is awake and being moved to a private room. I will let you know when she is settled." She stopped, turned her head back and forth, checking the hallway, then her voice lowered, "He also said to tell you that if you keep the noise down, he will allow more than two in her room at a time."

"Not a problem," said a few of us.

"Great, I will be back to tell you when you can see her." The nurse walked away.

"I'm going to call the Prez and let the club know she's awake," I said, pulling my phone out and stepping out of the room. Speed followed. I was sure it was to call Sami to update her on her friend and to share what Devil had told us.

As I walked down the hall waiting for Stroker to answer, it didn't escape my notice that, for the first time today, I could breathe easily. I planned to enjoy the feeling for however long it lasted.

When I heard Stroker pick up, I started speaking, "Hey, Dad. Got good news."

Chapter Nine

Carly

"Man, that one nurse was smoking hot. Think I can talk her into taking my temperature?"

"Yeah, Moose, maybe she will use a rectal one. That way you could feel like you were back in the joint." I heard a thud outside my room, and then male laughter followed it. I smiled to myself.

"Damn it, Keg, can't you boys go anywhere without causing problems? You are going to get us thrown out before we even get to check on her. I'm getting too old for this shit." Wild Bill had been saying that for as long as I could remember.

"If you fuckers don't be quiet, you aren't going in the damn room. She's been shot for fuck's sakes." My smile left. Who did Crusher think he was, bossy asshole?

"Seriously, brother, you need to tone it back, or you are going to get blue balls before she lets you touch her."

"Shut up, Flirt. At least I don't have to tie mine down to get them to fuc—" That thud was just outside the door. "What did you do that for?"

"Because your assholishness is showing, brother. She doesn't need that." The door started sliding open.

"You can see through yours enough to see mine, eh?" Speed was first in the door, followed by the others who were laughing.

"To think I thought you were good enough for my little sister." Speed smiled at me and then winked. I wanted to be annoyed, but his acceptance of me felt pretty fucking awesome.

"Can't take it back now. Others heard you, no giving me shit later." Crusher laughed and walked to the side of my bed. "Hey, baby, what's the face for? Are you in pain? Want me to call the nurse?" He reached for the call button on the rail. I just looked at him, I have no idea what the fuck happened while I was in surgery, but it was like I woke up in an alternate universe called hell. Why was he being so nice? Freaking weird.

"You touch that button, and I will slap your hand." Wild Bill came to the other side of my bed and leaned in, and kissed my cheek. I just shook the thoughts out of my head and then looked up at Wild Bill and smiled. When he rose up, he looked over to Crusher, shook his head, and laughed. Crusher was glaring at him. "Did I miss something while I was in surgery?" I looked between the two men. Someone better start talking, was all I thought as I watched the two men stare each other down. Holy crap, when Wild Bill was the first to break the stare, I was a little shocked. I mean, he was the biggest badass around, and yeah, Speed and the other Black Hawks were badasses, but Wild Bill had been around too long. He had perfected it.

"Not what you are thinking, girl. But I think your brother should be the one to tell you everything that happened after you blacked out at the gas station. The boys and I are going to head back to Haven. Got a little club business to take care of. You need us, you call. Hear me?" I nodded, and he bent back over and hugged me. Then he stepped back while Moose and Crank did the same. Crusher grunted and turned and walked out. I looked at the door when he pulled it shut behind him and frowned. The other Black Hawk men were chuckling, even my newfound brother. *Men*, I wondered if I would ever understand them.

"What is wrong with Crusher?" I looked up at Reed, who wore a huge grin.

"Ah, nothing for you to worry about. I think he suffers from not wanting to share his toys." Reed leaned over and hugged and kissed my forehead. When he stood back up, the grin was gone. "You take care of yourself, watch your back, and don't ever scare me like you did today. Call me if you need anything. I'll see you at Ally's birthday party if

I don't see you sooner. Speed said Sami was going to set one up for her. Prez and I will be down. Love ya, mouse."

"Love you too, butthead."

Wild Bill laughed and tilted his head to the door, and they moved toward it, but as they walked by Speed, who was standing to the side, Wild Bill stopped and shook his hand. When he reached the door the others had left open when they'd left, he said over his shoulder, "Don't forget, she was ours first," then he was gone.

Speed walked to the side of my bed and pulled up a chair, the others came to stand on the other side, and after some whispered voices in the hall, Crusher walked back in.

"So, what went on? What do you have to tell me?" I was starting to get tired, but I wanted to know everything first.

"Jag, Flirt, Devil, and Coast are going to head out. They just wanted to tell ya goodbye before they left," Speed said, and they stepped closer to the bed.

"And do it without touching you," Crusher finished, glaring at the men as they smiled back at him.

Jag and Coast patted my shoulder, told me to take care, then stepped back. Flirt stepped up, but instead of patting my shoulder, he winked and leaned down and kissed my cheek.

"Flirt." His name coming from Crusher was said like a warning, but it didn't seem to affect the man. He laughed and stepped back.

"You're going to do just fine. See you back home." After Flirt had moved out of the way, Devil moved closer, but before he could speak, I did.

"You're the one the doctor said saved my life. You were a medic in the Army, right?" When he smiled at me, it changed his whole look, which wasn't bad to begin with. It did answer where the name Devil came from. I imagined that look had gotten him into a lot of women's panties.

"Yeah, darlin', that's me. You're welcome anytime." He hugged me, and the four men walked out, leaving just me, Crusher, and Speed in the room.

I looked at Speed, "Start talking."

Speed started to talk, and Crusher pulled the other chair closer to my bed. I listened without interrupting as he told me everything that happened, even what Devil had figured out. I closed my eyes when he finished to absorb all he had said. Crusher and Speed said nothing while I laid there. When I started laughing and opened my eyes, Crusher and Speed were frowning as if I'd lost my mind. Hell, maybe I had.

"You okay?" Crusher asked.

"Sure am." I looked at Speed, "If my leg didn't hurt, I'd get out of this bed and freaking dance around the damn room. So much makes sense now. You have no idea."

"Tell us, baby," Crusher said.

"Not like we were ever your normal family, but in the beginning, Wallace treated me, I guess as a daughter. He'd take me places with him, bought me a bike on my fifth birthday, taught me to ride. They would both come to school shit, though I wished they wouldn't have because you could smell the liquor on him, and Clarice's eyes would always be bloodshot from whatever she was flying high on at the time. As I got older, I actually used to feel bad about not telling them when things were going on at school because I didn't want to be embarrassed. We spent a lot of time at the clubhouse, so I was around Sami and Reed daily. When they would want to go out or not deal with me, Wild Bill's house was where I stayed. What's worse is I didn't mind. I enjoyed the time away from them.

"At fourteen, it changed with Wallace. He was hateful when he spoke to me. He even made comments to Clarice in front of me about how he should never have made her his ol' lady. I was never at the house when his buddies would come over, the one your man Brax killed, Creeper, and another named Jacks, because they'd party to all hours, so those were times I'd stay with Sami. Keeping that away from me stopped too. One day I came home and walked into the trailer to Clarice straddling Jacks on the floor with Creeper in her mouth and Wallace taking her from behind. When I turned around to walk back out, Wallace said, *'You should stay and watch. You are your mother's daughter after all. Club whore is your future, girl.'*" I looked between Crusher and Speed, and the two sat with their hands clenched into fists in their laps.

"Did he or they ever touch you, baby?" Crusher gritted out.

"No." My single answer was at least enough for the two men to relax their hands while they sat waiting for me to continue. "After Clarice had overdosed, he drank more and more, and he would stay gone for days, then I would come home from school, and he would be there, back from wherever. Jacks and Creeper came over more often, and a few times, I was woken by loud voices because they would be fighting with each other. One night they were so loud that I could hear what they were arguing about, and from then on, I lived at Sami's. Wild Bill never questioned me there. I never told him what they said or what I had seen before."

"What were they talking about, Carly?" Speed's fists were balled up again.

"Jacks and Creeper were yelling at Wallace about how he promised I would be Clarice's replacement if they'd help him. They yelled they had done their part, now, he needed to deliver on his promise. Wallace told them to keep their dicks in their pants and that it was going to be soon. That's when I went to Sami's house and started staying there. I was around seventeen when Wild Bill found out about the takeover, and Wallace and the others took off."

Crusher whispered, "He's a dead man." I looked at him. He wore the same face Speed did, and his hands were balled into fists, too. I focused back and continued.

"So he knew, I don't know how and I don't care. I could dance because for years, I worked not to be them. I know Clarice left you, Speed, trust me, you got the better deal there. I got stuck with her, but it is nice to know Wallace isn't my dad. From what I hear, you got the best there, Speed."

"Thanks, Carly. And I understand, now you need to also. You never got to meet Cutter, our dad, but if he had

107

known about you, he would have done anything to get to you. There is a lot of him in you, and I just noticed that sitting here listening to you talk and watching your facial expressions. I'm sorry for everything you had to put up with, but I'm not sorry that all this has happened because it brought you here."

I wiped my eyes at his words. He was right. We had each other now, and fuck everything else. "Sami never had a chance, did she?" Speed smiled and got out of the chair, and hugged me. I looked over to Crusher, and he winked. Mentioning Sami reminded me, "Why are you here, Speed? Why didn't you leave when Sami called you today?"

"Because Sami and Ally had a club watching out for them, and you didn't. They're my family, Carly, but so are you." I could only nod. I was going to enjoy every minute of getting to know my brother.

"Speed's going to head back with the others, though, and I am going to stay here until you are released," Crusher said, and I looked at Speed.

"Coast and I will be back with a truck when you get released because there is no way you are going to be riding your bike for a while. You can ride in the truck, and then Coast can ride your bike back. Until then, you will be in good hands." Before I could do any protesting, Crusher and Speed did the man hug thing, and he was gone, and Crusher was back in the chair. My energy was gone, and my body was yelling sleep, but I couldn't stop staring at him, leaned back in the chair with his eyes closed.

"Get some rest, baby. I'll still be here when you wake, and you can yell at me then."

"You're an ass."

"I'm your ass. The sooner you accept that, the easier it will be."

I closed my eyes. He was right. I could yell at him tomorrow.

Chapter Ten

Crusher

Carly slept through the night if a little restlessly. Me, I dozed off and on; her every whimper had my eyes opening. I stayed in her room through the night and would continue to as long as she was here. That had been an argument with the floor nurse. One I won when Jag called the administration and informed them that I was Ms. Monroe's security and if they expected their rules to be followed, then they would need to sign the letter he would be glad to fax them saying they would take full responsibility if anything happened to Carly while in their care.

That was followed up by the local police captain's call informing them the shooter hadn't been apprehended and

Ms. Monroe could still be in danger. That was enough, and she was going to have to deal with it. The thought of them getting to her in the hospital was unacceptable.

I shifted and looked at her. She was beautiful, and I didn't give a shit if she protested. She *was* mine. Her eyes were closed, the soft breaths that were coming out of her mouth were tempting, and the little noises she made were cute.

Sometime in the middle of the night, I had had enough of the chair and moved to my current place of sharing Carly's bed. I'd laid down on the side, slid my arm under her, and shifted us to fit as comfortably as humanly possible in a bed made for one. Add in avoiding the IV line, and all was good. Thank fuck my girl was out, 'cause I had no doubt if she'd been woken up, there would have been an argument.

It wasn't long after I joined her in the bed that she curled into me, and I had slept the longest I had in one interval for months, only waking when her body would twitch, which I assumed was the pain making its presence known in her slumber. If I could take it all away for her, I would.

My only problem with the current situation was between her warm breath hitting my chest through my t-shirt and the small hand that started at my chest and rubbed back and forth and up and down, moving lower with each pass. My brain understood the woman beside me was injured and needed care, not mauled. However, my dick evidently missed that message or ignored it because its state of being trapped behind my zipper, jumping every damn time the hand moved closer, reminded me that I was the one who put us both in this situation, which only pissed me off.

The nurse came in, and I turned more toward Carly to hide the evidence of my arousal. Her frown gave away her knowledge of my predicament, her whispered words verified it.

"Remember, she needs to curb her activity while she heals. She can't get too worked up," the nurse said, then walked out of the room and pulled the door behind her.

The body beside me shook, and the face pressed harder into my chest so the laughter couldn't be heard.

"How long have you been awake?" I tightened my arm around her.

"How long have you been in my bed?" The woman I've known these months was back. I'd often wondered if she saw her own strength, her ability to see the light at the end, no matter if the beginning was dark. She found the positive in a situation, accepted the good, and didn't let the bad drag her down. She was mouthy, independent, and hardheaded, and I wanted her to be mine in body and soul. I was patient, steadfast, and determined. She hadn't had a chance. I just needed her to accept it.

"Not long enough, baby." She pinched my side.

"I meant now. I don't understand why you keep this up. We had sex, I walked out when I found out you were club because I'm not Sami. I don't want club life, Crusher. I've spent a lot of time untangling myself from it." She tried to untwine herself from me, and I wouldn't allow it. Her huffed breath showed her agitation.

"You're wrong, Carly. You may not want club life, but the club is embedded in you. Why do you think you ran to Haven? And finding out about Speed, accepting it so easily, everything you've done to this point shows different.

"You distanced yourself from Stone, even your mother, it wasn't because they were club, or you would never have gone to Sami's house. You were young, and the shit that went on around you was wrong, but it had nothing to do with the club, only the people. Fight it all you want, but MC life will always be a part of you that you can't get rid of.

"Are you going to give up Sami and Ally? Going to distance yourself from Speed because of his affiliation with Black Hawk? You can't have it both ways. You know it, and I know it, the difference—I've accepted club life and the part I will play in it—you haven't." I released her and got out of her bed.

"I'm not going to ignore Speed, but he is in the club. I'm not. It is the same with Sami and Ally, even the men at Haven. I went to Haven to find answers. I've built a life outside the club, Crusher, and you and no one else can make me return to it." She raised the bed, putting herself into a sitting position.

"Good to know about Speed, Sami, and Ally. And you didn't run to Haven for answers, Carly, it was because the men have been and are your family. As far as making you come into club life, you're right. No one can. But no one will have to either because you will do it on your own, just like

I'm not going to pressure you to be with me. That too will be because you want there to be an us."

"You are going to be waiting a long time if you think I am going to come to you."

"I'm patient, Carly. And while I'm letting you catch up with me, I will be waiting."

"Why, Crusher? Why are you doing all this? It was only one time. No one pushes so hard after one time with someone, so why?" Her frown told me she had no clue, she would, though.

"The first time was your body, but, baby, your strength is what keeps me coming back." I grabbed my bag and headed toward the bathroom in the room. Christ, I hoped it didn't take her long to catch up with me.

Chapter Eleven

Carly

When the bathroom door closed behind him, tears came. I didn't cry. I never cried. But what he said, OMG, who wouldn't cry? The door pushed open, and the nurse came in with my tray and meds until I saw her; my leg pain hadn't even registered. I wiped my eyes as she moved to the side of my bed, sat the tray down, and handed me the cup that held the pills. I swallowed them down, and then she did her thing: blood pressure, temperature, looking at the bandage, and checking to see if the wrap wasn't too tight. She gathered her things and then looked at me.

"Sweetie, my Elliot, he pursued me relentlessly, and it took a good year before I would even go out with him. If he had said something like your young man just did at any time during his pursuit, I would have been the one to drag him to the altar because I would have been afraid that he would wake up one day and think me not worthy. Men like yours don't come around every day, those are the ones you just hold onto and let them take you on the ride of your life."

"But why put up with a bossy, bullhead man who plows over you?" She smiled, then bent closer.

"Because it's a powerful feeling when they focus it all on you. There is nothing better than young love, hon. Well, maybe old lovin'."

"Oh, we aren't in love," I said, and she winked and walked toward the door.

"Denial is a wonderful thing." She chuckled and pulled the door closed.

When Crusher came out of the bathroom, I was eating my breakfast. He placed his bag back in the corner, then informed me he was going down to the cafeteria to grab a coffee and some breakfast for himself and that he would be back in a bit. The door closed, and he was gone, and I suddenly felt alone.

After I had finished eating, they'd returned to help me clean up and put on a new gown, then they took the tray away. What I would give for my t-shirt and shorts I usually slept in. The doctor came in no sooner than I was back in bed. He asked questions about my pain level, un-bandaged my thigh, and checked out his work when it came time to tell me how long I would have to stay at the hospital, Crusher walked in.

"Doc, how is she?" Crusher said and walked to the opposite side of the bed the doctor was on.

"Wound looks good for just a day after surgery. It helps, Ms. Monroe, that you are young and in good shape. Your healing time will be more expedient than for someone older. I will release you the day after tomorrow as long as there is no seepage, and your pain stays moderate. When you are back in your hometown, you will need to check in with your doctor there so he can continue to monitor your recovery and inform you when you will be able to start therapy. And before you argue that it is not going to be necessary, I will tell you it will be. The muscle will have to be built back from lack of use. Do you have any questions, Ms. Monroe?"

"How soon will I be able to go back to work?" I hoped it wasn't out too long, I had some savings to tide me over but not for an extended time.

"At least a month, and after your doctor feels you can return, it will be to light duty."

"You mean behind a desk?" Damn, if that wouldn't be some boring shit.

"Ms. Monroe, though your injury is now on the mend, it was a very serious injury you sustained. The femoral was nicked. If it had been larger in size, we wouldn't be having this conversation." I looked at Crusher, who was staring back at me. I nodded and then thanked the doctor, never taking my eyes off Crusher. He broke the eye contact and shook the doctor's hand, asking a few questions of his own that I didn't pay attention to because I was busy thinking of everything I could have lost or never experienced. Crusher was at the top of the list.

Crusher turned back to me, and his eyebrows drew together, "You hurting, baby?"

"No, just tired. Will you um...lay with me?" He didn't answer my question; he just moved to my uninjured side and laid down, pulling me into his arms. I laid my head on his chest and let his heartbeat lull me to sleep.

Chapter Twelve

Crusher

"I'm not staying at your house. I'll be fine on my own." Carly argued again.

The last two days at the hospital had been relaxing. We talked, laughed, and really got to know each other. I told her about my time in the Army, she told me stories about growing up at Haven. We told each other the most basic stuff, like favorite colors, foods, cars, bikes, and even sports. My girl liked football. I asked why and she said without pause that nothing beat a butt in those uniform pants. She even laughed at me when I growled.

At night I laid down with her, and she curled into me as if we'd been sleeping like that for years. I'd slept too and felt rested and more energized than I had even before going into the military.

Carly smiled when the guys showed up with the truck. She'd even joked with Coast about riding her bike. She'd been so agreeable the last two days that I'd wondered if I'd lost my feisty girl. Then after an hour in the truck, she was back, I couldn't hold in the grin. This side of my woman had me shifting a little in the driver's seat. Being a gentleman and giving her the time to heal could possibly kill me.

"Are you even listening to me, Crusher? You're going home, and I am staying at my place. There is no need for you to stay with me. And why the fuck are you grinning?"

Oh yeah, I may have to stop at the next exit and take care of my problem, I reached down and pulled at the crotch of my jeans, anything to give my swelling dick more room.

"Oh my God, do you have a hard-on? Put that sucker away. How can you even think of that when I am yelling at you?" I glanced over, and she was staring at my crotch, which didn't help one bit because the bastard liked her eyes on him even if it was behind the jeans.

"You don't need to be alone, it would be easier for me if you stayed at my house so I could work at the shop without having to drive to Black Hawk, but I will do it for you. Do you need to stop? Are you hurting or want something to drink, baby?"

"Stop being so nice. Where is the grouchy man who barks orders at me? At least then I could have a decent argument and not feel like I am talking to myself."

"Come here." I laid my one arm over the back of the seat so she could scoot in the middle, and with the Escalade's bench seat, she'd be able to prop her leg up on the seat. She looked at my arm and then back to my crotch.

"I'm not getting anywhere close to that, it might break free, and I will be trapped."

"You didn't complain when he was tucked in behind your ass in the hospital. You got more on now than you did there. He was riding your crack since the hospital gown had no back and you weren't wearing any panties, which brings me to ask why since I brought your saddlebags in the room with your extra clothes."

"I told you I didn't wash them at Wild Bill's house. The ones in there were dirty."

I looked over at her again and grinned.

"Stop it, there is nothing funny." She crossed her arms over her chest and turned her face to look out the window.

We rode for a while in the quiet until Speed rode up beside the truck and signaled they wanted to stop. I nodded, and he dropped back.

"Good, we are stopping. I need to use the restroom."

"I would have stopped at any time if you had said something instead of pouting."

"I'm not pouting."

"Yes, you are."

"No, I'm not."

I burst out laughing, and she turned toward me. I glanced over at her while I pulled to a stop at the bottom of the exit.

"You, baby, make a terrible patient." Her lips twitched, and her eyes shined.

"No, I'm not." And she couldn't hold it any longer and laughed. The honk of a horn had me looking in the rearview mirror at the others with their hands held up in the 'what the fuck' sign. I rolled down the window, turned toward the gas station, and simultaneously flipped them off. I couldn't remember the last time I had this much fun on a road trip. The only thing I regretted was the circumstances that placed us there.

I pulled to the front of the place so Carly didn't have far to walk and parked. I watched her as she made her way into the store.

"Fuckin' A. Another one is down," Coast said, standing by my window.

"I think so, man," I said, then turned to look at him when Carly was out of sight.

"She's doing well considering it's only been three days. She'll make a good ol' lady for a president, brother." Coast was always on duty, his eyes scanning the parking lot as he talked.

"Yeah, I just have to get her to believe." The door to the store opened, and Carly and Speed walked out, laughing at something. The passenger door opened, and Carly was preparing to use the step to lift herself in when Speed grabbed her waist and hoisted her up as if she weighed nothing.

"You have to stop doing that. I can get in on my own." She glared at Speed, and he glared back.

"I don't have to do shit, you on the hand need to let people help you. And why didn't you get out, Crusher, and help her in?"

"'Cause I knew you would do it, and why should I get the backlash when I could put that on you." Carly looked between us and buckled her seatbelt.

"Both of you are asses." Speed closed the door chuckling.

"I'm not sure I like having a sister. Glad she is your problem."

"Oh please, you are enamored by my greatness." Speed looked at her and just shook his head, then he reached in the window and rubbed the top of her head.

"Sure, little sis, keep believing that." I watched as she flipped Speed off as he walked away. Watching the two made me wonder how much would have been different around Black Hawk if those two had grown up together.

"And stop calling me that!" Carly stuck her head out the window and yelled across the parking lot. Speed's reply was to give her the one finger wave over his shoulder.

"Dude, the clubhouse is never going to be the same," Coast said and, not waiting for a reply, turned toward his bike. Once they were mounted and ready to go, we pulled back onto the road for the last leg of the trip.

"Why are we heading to Sami's old house? I haven't moved all my stuff there yet," Carly said as I pulled into the drive. Speed pulled in behind me. Coast had headed back to Black Hawk instead of following to the house.

"The club moved you in, and Sami oversaw it. They got your stuff in, put away, and I imagine the ol' ladies have stocked the refrigerated full with stuff. Probably won't have to cook for a month." I got out and walked around as she pushed her door open. I helped her out, and the door opened when I set her on her feet, and Ally ran out with Sami behind her.

"Aunt Carly, you are my daddy's sister!"

"Ally cat! Yes, I am." I caught Ally just before she was going to launch herself at Carly, who stood with her arms open to catch her.

"Baby, you can't do that. Walking is it for you right now. No carrying anything that will put extra weight on your leg." I hoisted Ally on my shoulders, and she giggled.

"Ally, didn't we have a talk about being watchful around Aunt Carly until she's healed?" Sami spoke while she and Carly hugged.

"Yep, I was watching around her, and I didn't see anything. Momma, I need a sister like Daddy." Speed chuckled and lifted Ally from my shoulders to place her on his. He didn't catch the look on Sami's face after Ally spoke, but I did.

"Your momma meant watching, so you don't do anything to Aunt Carly because of her leg. No diving on her." Speed patted Ally's leg.

"Come on, let's get you inside. You're probably tired." Sami stuck her arm through Carly's and led her into the house.

"Sami is going to help get her settled, and then we are going to head to the house. The trip wore on her, she looks tired." Speed looked back at the house.

"Yeah, last hour was hard on her. She was fidgety, so I figure sitting in the car has that leg pretty painful right now, but she never said a word."

"Did you tell her?" I smiled at Speed's question.

"Tell what, Daddy?" Ally leaned over Speed's head to look at him upside down, and he grabbed her shoulders and flipped her to the ground. She laughed and took off into the house.

"No, she'll figure it out soon enough."

Speed smirked and shook his head. "You know she is going to go off on you, right?"

I nodded. "Yeah, I like it." Speed groaned, and Sami and Ally walked out the front door.

"Aunt Carly is in bed. Momma said she needs sleep to get better before my party. I'm having a cookout, you comin'?"

"I'll be there, Spider. What do you want for your birthday?" I asked.

"I want a bike."

"You have a bike, Ally," Sami answered.

"Not a bike with pedals. A bike like Daddy's." Sami popped Speed on the shoulder, and Speed looked down at Ally.

"Baby, we talked about this. Momma said you're too small for one. Maybe for your sixth birthday. Okay?"

"Alright, but I'm gonna have to tell Uncle Reed because I told him I wanted one." The heavy breath she let out as if saying 'what a chore' was too cute. Speed's groan said this had been an ongoing discussion.

"I will kill him if he buys one," Sami said, and Ally, who had her men wrapped around her finger, always took up for us.

"But, I would be sad, Momma, if you killed Uncle Reed. He loves me." Her lips came out in a pout, and she looked up at her mom, and her eyes looked as if she were going to cry. This club was so doomed.

"Fine, Uncle Reed lives another day. Let's go home and let Uncle Crusher and Aunt Carly get settled." Sami grabbed Ally's hand after telling me bye and Speed that she would get Ally buckled in.

"Call if you need anything, and we will cover you at the shop. Take as much time as you need to take care of her. Bring her to the house to visit if she needs to get out. Don't forget Sue is next door. Rooting for you, brother, and good luck." Speed gave me a man hug and chuckled. "You could do what I did, give her a deadline."

"I could, but she will come to me on her own." He slapped my back and headed to Sami's car across the street. I watched them pull away, and then I pushed Carly's bike into the small garage before going into the house. Speed and Coast had switched out at the gas station so Coast could ride my bike to the house.

I checked on Carly, and she was sound asleep. She'd already kicked the blankets off, I learned that was her thing at the hospital. We'd start out under them, and then I would wake up cold, and the blankets would be piled at the bottom of the bed. She was slightly pale, her face relaxed in sleep, and her blonde hair spread out across the pillow.

She was going to be mad when she woke and found me here. But she'd get over it. I looked at her tank top and shorts she wore and wondered if she had put on any panties. I knew for a fact the panties she had in her saddlebags were clean because I had looked in the bag when I brought them into the hospital room. My baby had been horny even dealing with pain, she'd thought I'd been asleep when she backed her ass into me and wiggled until I was flush up against her. But I would never do anything that would put her at risk. I was here to take care of her, I could wait to make her mine.

I put away the stuff from the saddlebags and headed to the shower, she'd sleep for a bit if she had taken the painkillers the doctor prescribed.

Chapter Thirteen

Carly

The smell of food had my eyes opening, and then I heard the TV playing as I lay in bed. I just started to rise when the bedroom door opened, and Crusher walked in, carrying a tray.

"Good, you're awake. You need to take your pain meds, but need to eat something first." I listened and watched as he set the tray on the nightstand and grabbed the pill bottle, shaking a couple out and holding out his hand for me to take them.

"How long was I asleep?" I asked, then popped the pills and reached for the glass of water on the tray.

"'Bout six hours. You were worn out from the drive, your body needed the rest. Now here, eat, and you will feel better." He grabbed the tray and held it out to me.

"Hold that thought. Bathroom first." I gingerly threw my legs over the bed and sat up.

"Let me help you." He set the tray back down, then grabbed my waist, lifting me to a standing position.

"I would have gotten up on my own. Why are you here? Don't you have a house?" I knew that was bitchy, but my thigh was hurting, and he was being sweet. I didn't want sweet, it reminded me of my injury. I wanted the Crusher I could spar with verbally to take my mind off the pain.

"I told you I was going to take care of you. Would have been more convenient at my house, but this is what you wanted." I made my way to the bathroom and entered, closing the door behind me.

Fine. He'd get tired of driving up and down the road and stop coming by. I did my business and, on the way out, stopped to look in the mirror. I shouldn't have. There were dark circles under my eyes, my skin was pale, and my hair looked as if birds had made a nest in it. I needed a shower, I felt gross and ugly. Well, that should make him leave. I walked out of the bathroom to Crusher leaning back on the bed, the tray resting on his lap.

"What are you doing?" I asked as I sat on the side of the bed and swung my good leg up, then, with care, put my hands under my thigh and lifted my other leg onto the bed.

"Sitting here to make sure you eat."

"I can't sit that on my leg." Instead of answering me, he reached to the bottom of the tray and pulled the bars down so the tray would sit up on my lap. After positioning it across me, he leaned back and turned on the TV.

"Now eat," he said while flipping channels.

"Bossy much," I muttered, picked up the spoon, and dipped it in the soup.

"Not if you do what I tell you to do." He turned and winked at me.

I ate, and he watched TV, neither of us said a word. When I was done, I folded the legs on the tray, set it on the nightstand, and then leaned back in bed. We remained that way for a while. I watched Crusher out of the corner of my eye, and he looked relaxed as he lounged. He wore gym shorts and nothing else. His chest was tanned and bare. The only hair started just under his belly button and disappeared into the waistband of his pants. Both his arms held tattoos from shoulder to elbow, and the only other tattoo I knew was on his body was on his back, it was the Black Hawk MC emblem. He was muscled and fit, and if I closed my eyes, I could almost imagine the feel of his skin.

"You getting tired again, baby?" I startled and opened my eyes.

"Umm...a little, but I want a shower and to wash my hair. I feel gross."

"You're beautiful, baby," Crusher said, got off the bed, and walked around to help me. This time I put my hand out for him to help me. I lost my balance, and he caught me and held me against him, my hands splayed against his chest.

133

When I looked up at him, the brown of his eyes was darker and focused on my mouth. He leaned down and captured my mouth with his, and the kiss was tender at first, then his tongue licked across my lower lip, and I opened my mouth, his tongue entering, the kiss deepening. One of Crusher's hands grabbed my waist while the other went into the hair at the back of my head, and he held me to him. I was lost in the kiss, lost in him. The pain in my leg was forgotten as he took what he wanted but gave me more than I thought I could ever feel. I'd kissed Crusher before, but this was different. It was a kiss with a message, one I didn't know if I was ready to answer.

I moved my hands over his chest, his shoulders, and back, again the warmth of his skin was comforting. As my body melted into his and my legs grew weak, he broke the kiss and leaned his forehead against mine. We stared into each other's eyes while we caught our breaths. He was the first to recover, and he steadied me and stepped back.

"The doctor said you could take the bandage off, just don't rub the area with a cloth or anything, just to let the water flow over it until you get the stitches out. I'll call the doctor and set up an appointment to remove the stitches." While he talked, he got me clothes out of the drawers, then walked into the bathroom, and I heard the shower start before I moved out of the spot I was standing in.

"Okay, I can handle it from here." I retrieved a towel out of the cabinet and put it on the counter.

"I'll be in the bedroom if you need me. Sit on the bench and use the sprayer so you don't slip." Crusher walked out and pulled the door closed behind him.

After taking the bandage off and my clothes, I got in the shower and let the water run over me. I washed and conditioned my hair, then washed my body. Spotting the razor, I looked down at my legs, they could use a shaving among other parts. After the last few swipes of the razor, I rinsed again, stood, and shut the water off.

"You okay in there," Crusher's voice came through the door.

"Yes, just finishing up," I yelled back as I stepped out of the shower. I dried off, only patting the skin over the wound. By the time I put my clothes on and wrapped a towel around my wet hair, I was exhausted. When I entered the bedroom, Crusher sat on the end of the bed with a fresh bandage and the tube of cream the doctor had given me.

"Get comfortable on the bed, and I'll fix you up." When I was in place, he sat on the side and laid the items down in the order he wanted them. "Feel better now?"

"Yes, and the sprayer was nice. When did that get put in?" When Sami had brought me into the house, I had been shocked even after Crusher had told me the club had moved me in. Everything was put away, not a box in sight, and he had been right about the refrigerator too. The members' ol' ladies had it full with food. It humbled me.

"Flirt, he's good with his hands." He had the tube open and gently began to apply the cream.

"I heard." Crusher chuckled at my words. "Women talk."

"I bet they do." His head was bent as he concentrated on what he was doing.

"Yeah, I never saw so many happy women around town until you guys came home." I chuckled, and his head snapped up, and he looked at me and stopped what he was doing.

"Carly, I've slept with a lot of women. I'm not going to deny that. But I don't want to talk about them. You're the only woman I've slept with who had any effect on me. Once I met you, the others no longer mattered." He bent his head back down and finished applying the bandage as I watched, speechless. I would think back to this moment later on and realize it was when I fell in love. Just not now, I wanted to remain in my world of denial.

Crusher

After taking the tray down, I made sure the house was locked up and headed back upstairs. When she started talking about the women in town, I couldn't help but feel a little pissed that we'd been gossiped about, but then that quickly passed. It's not like we didn't share the info if a woman was easy or had a little kink to her. We'd shared girls growing up. But women had meant one thing to me before, a means to obtain a release. Was I proud of that? No. Do I regret any of it? No. I never forced or hurt a woman I had been with, and when I walked away, I left them exhausted, pleasured, and with a smile on their face.

I walked into the bedroom, and she was stretched out with her eyes closed. "You take your pills again?" I asked as I moved to the empty side of the bed.

"Uh huh, you can go home now. It's getting late." She never opened her eyes, only spoke. I didn't answer her. I folded back the covers and laid down on the bed. Her head turned, and her eyes opened.

"What are you doing?"

"You didn't want to come to my house, so I am staying here."

"You don't need to stay here and take care of me." While she talked, I scooted over and slid my arm under her, and pulled her to me. She placed her head on my chest and reached down, and pulled the covers over us. We'd turned the lamp off while we watched TV earlier, so I grabbed the remote I had on the table beside me and flipped it off, throwing the room into darkness.

"Told you before, I got you, and I'm not going anywhere."

"You can't push yourself into my life and make me do what you want." I could feel her yawn against my chest as she threw her arm across my stomach.

"Carly? Carly?" I received no response from her. Smiling into the darkness, I closed my eyes. "I already have, baby. You just haven't realized it."

Chapter Fourteen

Carly

Ten days! Ten days of touching me, kissing me, rubbing my legs as they were draped over his lap as we sat on the couch. Every night listening to his heartbeat as my head rested on his chest. Waking up wrapped in his arms with the feel of his erection pushing up against me, only to have him kiss my forehead and get out of bed. Yeah, it had been the longest ten days of my life and the most frustrating. I had always been active, having it taken away had been hard. Add in an insufferable man with his: eat, take your medicine, you can't lift that, you aren't supposed to do that, made for long days of nothing. The frustration, I wanted Crusher with everything in me, but no, the man wouldn't break. If he didn't fuck me soon, I planned to get my vibrator out and use it while I lay next to him.

"What's the frown for, your leg hurting?" Like he didn't know. For the past week, I did everything but climb him like a tree. But if I'd done that, he would have only yelled that was too much motion. Crusher sat in the chair across from the exam table I was currently laid out on while we waited for the doctor to come in and remove the stitches from my thigh. He was relaxed and looked comfortable in his skin. I, on the hand, was sure an alien was going to pop out from under mine if someone so much as touched me. The man had me wounded so tight I felt like I could explode any minute.

"No. Just a dull ache," I answered and then under my breath added, "in my crotch." I knew Crusher heard me when he chuckled, but before I could snap at him, the exam room door opened, and the doctor walked in.

"How are you doing, Ms. Monroe?"

"Better once these stitches get out and you tell me I can go back to work or at least resume some activities." See, wound tight.

"Someone's not been a very good patient?" The doctor would see good if he didn't get on with it.

"She's not been too bad, doc. Just suffering some tightness in a couple of places," Crusher said, looked at me, and smirked. Asshole.

"Nice to hear, it means the skin is sealing closed. Also tells me you haven't had a lot of motion, which is good, less chance of rupture by keeping the pressure off it." The doctor looked down at my chart, and I looked over at Crusher.

"But I need some motion, doc. I'm going to combust if I don't get any." Crusher's lips twitched.

"Well, let's get those stitches out then." I laid back on the table and closed my eyes as the probing and prodding when on. It wasn't long until he was finished, and I was sitting up listening to him talk to me about therapy. "I will set up your therapy to start in two weeks. Though the incision area looks great, you still need to take it relatively easy. The vein and muscle are on the mend but aren't one hundred percent. I'll also want to see you back in two weeks after your first therapy appointment. If all goes well, we'll see about getting you back to the sheriff's station. Until then, I'm recommending that you continue on your leave of absence.

"If you don't have any questions, I'll leave you to give the front desk your chart to get those appointments set up," the doctor finished, and when I didn't have any questions, he was out the door.

"Baby, that was good news," Crusher said and helped me down off the table.

"I know it is. And I know I am lucky, too. But, Crusher, I am going crazy with nothing to do."

"Yeah, baby, we need to see if we can find you an activity to do to burn off some of that energy." I didn't even respond as we stopped at the desk, got the receptionist's appointment cards, and headed to the parking lot. After getting in the truck, it didn't take long for us to get back to the house.

"I'm going to have a beer, and if you so much as tell me I can't because I am taking pain meds. I swear, Crusher, I will get my gun and shoot you. I won't even get sent to jail, it will be written off as a sexually frustrated woman who snapped and killed the closest man. No female juror would convict me."

Crusher laughed and reached into his pocket for his ringing phone. He looked at the screen and hit the talk button. "If you aren't going to talk, then quit calling my fucking number." Crusher disconnected the call. "Baby, Sami is supposed to stop by. When she gets here, I am going to run to Black Hawk and have Coast see what he can find out on this caller."

"Have you gotten a lot of them?" I knew he had gotten at least two while he was here taking care of me.

"About once a month for a couple of months, and now it seems we are down to weekly. I don't know who it is. One time a woman did ask if I was Russell Davis. But when I asked who she was and why she wanted to know, she hung up."

"Not a long, lost girlfriend?" I joked, but Crusher just stared at me, walked toward me, and then placed a hand on each side of my face. With his eyes locked with mine, he bent, and his mouth met mine, and the only thought I had was 'don't stop' as he devoured me. His tongue pressed in and met mine, and our combined tastes were intoxicating.

Crusher's hands moved from my face to travel down my arms and back up. He rubbed down my back until he reached my butt, and then he picked me up, the skirt I wore bunched up, and I wrapped my legs around him. He was gentle as he moved one of his hands off my butt to support my bad leg from underneath. Then my back hit the wall, and he pressed his erection into my center. I shifted my hips, and he groaned into my mouth, followed by my own moan when he rotated his hips, and the hardness of his jean-covered cock slid across my panty-covered pussy, and the friction had an orgasm building within me.

The kiss broke, and Crusher began a journey down my neck with his lips, stopping in the crease where my neck met my shoulder, then his teeth scraped over my skin, and I exploded. The orgasm hit with such force it left me lightheaded, my vaginal wall contracting. I shook in Crusher's arms, and then before I could fully comprehend, I was up in his arms as he walked toward the couch and sat me down.

I looked up into his eyes, and the glow of desire reflected back at me. I reached for him, taking hold of his pants' waist and pulling him closer. I reached for the zipper, and he placed his hand over mine, stopping my movement.

"I hear Speed's motorcycle coming, and trust me, we don't have time." He stepped back, and my hands dropped. "When I get inside you again, it will be a while before I come out. Rest up while I'm gone. You're going to need every ounce of endurance you can gather." The doorbell rang, and Crusher opened the door and said hi to Sami as she walked in.

Crusher walked back to me and kissed my forehead. "I'll be back in just a bit." Then he was gone, and Sami stood in front of me.

"Your face is flushed, and Crusher ran out of here as if his pants were on fire." Sami gave me that knowing look. When that happened in our youth, I learned how to deflect.

"Where is Spider bug? How come she didn't come with you today?" I sat on the couch, my legs stretched out. Ally had come with Sami every time they came to visit.

"She wanted to stay at the house. More specifically, the garage. The construction crew is putting up the extension, and Flirt, Jag, Coast, and Devil are overseeing that while working on the bike they have started. I didn't want to leave her with all that was going on, but the guys said it was alright and that every girl needed to know how to work on a bike. My daughter is turning into a miniature biker bitch." I laughed.

"Oh, it can't be that bad." I laughed harder at the look on Sami's face.

"Please, I forgot to tell you. When you were at Haven, Stroker and the other dads came back from their last trip. They brought her home a pair of leather pants, a leather vest, and black boots. Girl, I didn't even know they made that stuff that small. And for men, they got the sizes right."

Tears were running down my cheeks just imagining Ally dressed in the biker clothing. "Sami, you have lost the princess title."

Sami rolled her eyes, she had always hated when the men at Haven called her that. "That girl has them wrapped around her finger. Carly, we both know women are accepted in the clubs, but they have no say in how it is run, nor are they in the leadership. I don't want her to get hurt."

"Speed won't let that happen. And neither will Crusher, Sami."

"Listen to you. Where's the girl who wanted no part of club life?" Sami cocked her eyebrow in question.

"She got a refresher course on what family is about." I looked down at the pinkish scar on my leg.

"Carly, he's good for you. Not that you asked me, but I thought I would tell you anyway." Sami smiled.

I loved Sami like a sister. We've shared happy times and sad. "But am I good for him? That's the question." Sami shook her head at me.

"You've told me over the last two weeks everything you wouldn't share before. Carly, you rose above that shit, don't allow that to stop you from continuing to rise. Crusher is going to be the president of Black Hawk, his ol' lady is going to have to be strong and willful in her own right. Crusher sees that in you. I see it in you. It's time for you to see it in yourself." My eyes filled with tears again, and Sami came over and hugged me.

"He hasn't said anything about making me his ol' lady. This could be just a fling for him." Sami stood and literally doubled over laughing, and I frowned at her.

"Oh God, that felt good to laugh like that," Sami said after she got herself under control. "What do you think he's been doing? Huh, Carly?" She spread her arms out, "Here with you. The hospital. Everything from the time you left to go to Haven till now. What has he been doing?"

"He's been taking care of me, that's all."

"Oh my God, you really don't know. Did you expect him to give you an ultimatum like Speed gave me? He has maneuvered you. He might ask you to be his ol' lady, but Carly, you have been that since he stayed with you at the hospital. He let you have your say, then if he thought it wouldn't harm you, he gave you your way. If he didn't like what you wanted to do, he worked it until it was something he could accept.

"You accepted Speed as your brother with no question. Accept what is between you and Crusher. Don't analyze it. Just go with it."

Sami was right, it was time to carve out my own piece of happiness. "Speaking of Speed, why didn't he come in with you? Or did he have club business he needed to handle?"

"He visits Cutter's grave when he needs to talk things out. He told me he's done it since he got back. It helps him. He loved Cutter. Since I've been around the six of them more, I noticed underneath the tough, badass biker/ex-military men they are, there are six men who love as hard as they live. And if you are the woman they have chosen, there won't be a day that goes by that they won't show you that you mean everything to them. Once you are taken into their fold, they will protect you with everything they have. They are who writers make stories about. Carly, we used to read those romance books with my mom, remember?" At my nod, she continued, "Now we get to live it instead of reading about it."

"How'd you get so smart, Sami?" I smiled, and so did she. "Will you help me pack a few things to take to Crusher's house?"

"Yes. I'm so happy for you, Carly." We both stood and headed toward the stairs. "And before we head there, will you take me to Cutter's grave? I think I'd like to meet my dad."

"Carly, are you supposed to be doing so much on your leg?" Sami pulled Crusher's truck off to the side behind Speed's bike.

"I'm not putting any stress on it. I'll be fine." Sami stayed in the truck, and I got out and walked toward the lone figure that was knelt down on his heels in front of the black granite headstone. Speed must have heard my approach because he stood but didn't turn around. As I walked up next to him, I read what was written on the headstone.

"Cutter"

Harvey Paul Weston

Born – May 15, 19--

Died – Feb. 29, 20--

"Cutter would have loved you, Carly."

"Will you tell me about him, Speed?" I stepped closer, put my arm around his waist, and he placed his around my shoulder.

We stood together in front of our father's grave as Speed told me about Cutter from the first time he could actually remember him. We laughed, we cried, and we stood as brother and sister and grieved—him for the loss of a man he loved—and me for the loss of a man I never got the chance to love.

When we turned to leave, we left behind any regret for the time lost and took with us the celebration of the time we had left.

Chapter Fifteen

Crusher

"What do you mean, nothing?" I asked Coast as he continued to hit the keys on one crazy ass computer setup.

"Exactly that. I tracked it as far as Georgetown. It bounces back to Washington, DC, then over to Virginia, up to Maryland, and back again. It is stuck in some loop and hits a wall when you trace the number back." Coast frowned at his screen. How he knew what that shit meant was way past my knowledge of computers.

"Can you break through the wall?"

"Eventually, but it will take some time. Not going to have a quick answer on this one, Crusher. Whoever the lady is that keeps calling, she's got connections." Coast typed a bunch of codes in, hit enter, and pushed the chair back to stand. "I'll let that program run, might take a day or two before it returns anything useful. I'll keep checking and let you know. Other than to bring me your phone, what're you doing at Black Hawk when you should be locking down your woman."

"Don't worry about my woman. She's been locked down, it just hasn't hit her yet. Plus, I wanted to check in with my dad. He and I had been going over some of the club business and books, past and present, but with all the shit going on, I haven't gotten to sit down with him lately." Coast nodded. He knew exactly what I had been doing, he'd been doing the same with his dad, Cruz. We all had, and each one of the dads was responsible for some aspect of the MC. No one man would ever be able to keep up with everything it took to keep a club running smoothly. Especially one Black Hawk's size. For a club that started with six members, it had grown steadily over the years, reaching as high as fifty members at a given time. Men come, and men go, some just looking for a place to call home. Black Hawk had picked up members from the area when they moved in. Men who enjoyed the comradery liked to ride motorcycles and were looking for the loyalty and support of a brotherhood.

"Fair enough, but watch when it does hit her, she carries a gun." Coast laughed as we walked out of his house.

"Nah, I locked that up when we got back. A tempered woman, a gun, and the authority to fire it is not a good combination." We reached the garage behind Speed's place, and as we walked in, Coast and I both stopped to stare at the sight.

Flirt, Jag, and Devil sat on the floor with Ally, each with their head bent down over a carburetor with other parts and tools spread around them. But what stopped us was Ally's appearance. She was covered in grease.

"Shit, Sami is going to kill you." I walked over and looked down at them. Coast stood beside me, his head shaking back and forth.

"Sami knows Spider was going to help us today. We are showing her the working parts of the carburetor, she was in charge of greasing them." Flirt shrugged his shoulders like no big deal.

"Uh...did she bathe in the grease?" Ally looked up at Coast, and he began laughing

"Dudes, you are in so much trouble." The guys stood at Coast's words, and when Ally stood, and I got the full view of her, I laughed, too. Her black hair was in a ponytail, with sections that had come out of the band that was holding it off her face. Black marks were streaked on her face, and the parts of her arms, not covered by the t-shirt she wore, were in no better shape than her face. Sami would be better off burning the little girl's clothes than trying to wash them. But the smile on Ally's face might be the only thing that would keep Speed from joining in on Sami's murders.

"Uncle Crusher, Uncle Coast, look at my work. I'm helping put the carbeaters together." Ally's excitement was contagious.

"I see that. How'd you get all that grease on you?" I asked, and she looked down at herself as if she didn't know there was anything on her. Then she ran her hands down her shirt and jeans as if to dust off what she found. When she raised her head back up and looked at me, her hands went to her face, and she pushed the loose strands of hair out of the way, smearing what grease she had on her hands across her face.

"I helped Uncle Devil change the oil in his bike." She gave me the look of 'duh,' and I looked at Devil, who just smirked.

Yeah, we'd see how long the brother would keep that look when the momma stood in front of him.

"Nice knowing you, fucker," Coast said, and I smacked him in the chest. We at least made an attempt to clean up our language when the kid was around. But when I looked back at her, waiting for her usual response when foul language was used, she had her hands held out. One in my direction and the other in Coast's direction. When she spoke, I understood why we didn't get corrected.

"Uncle Jag said that I could get cash for not ratting out the men when they said bad words. See." She put her hand in her pocket and pulled out what looked like about five ones, then shoved them back in her pocket and held the hand she used back out to me. "I got that just from Uncle Jag 'cause he hurt his finger working on the bike and said a whole bunch of bad words." I looked at Jag, and he shrugged.

"Look at it this way. Speed and Sami won't have to come up with a shitload of cash for college." I couldn't argue there, but I wasn't going to stick around for the fireworks, so I dug into my pocket, pulled out a dollar bill, and handed it over. Coast did the same thing, and we watched Ally look at the bills as if she was checking to see if they were fake, and then she smiled and shoved them in her pocket. Black Hawk's own little shyster.

"I'm out. Going to see Stroker at the clubhouse. Nice knowing you dumbasses." I headed for the door. "Spider, I don't have any more ones. I'll have to owe you."

"Hey, you aren't going to help us? How are we supposed to get her cleaned up," Flirt yelled.

"My suggestion. A strip down on the porch and scrub in the shower." I walked out and didn't look back, but I did laugh at the panicked voices yelling behind me.

"We can't bathe a little girl!"

I approached the door to Stroker's office and knocked. The muffled voices I heard in the office quieted.

"Who is it?" Stroker yelled.

"Just me, Prez." I heard shuffling noises, and then Flyboy, Jag's dad and VP, opened the door to me. I walked in, and Stroker sat at the table in the back of the room with Cruz, Romeo, and Preacher. On the table were files spread out. It didn't escape me that Flyboy didn't sit back down but continued to stand by the door.

"Need something, Crusher?" Stroker asked as he closed the file in front of him.

"Checking in. Had some time if you wanted to go over some things. I can get the others to come over from the garage to help with whatever mess is in front of you." With the number of files spread out, I wondered if we had any issues going on with any of the club's businesses.

"No, you boys do whatever you got going on. We got this covered." The others looked at Stroker and then back at me. I could take a fucking hint, so I turned back toward the door.

"Call if you need me." I walked passed Flyboy, and he started to close the door.

"Crusher?" I stopped and turned back around. "The ol' ladies and Daisy are cooking stuff for a cookout for tomorrow after Church. Let the others know."

I didn't reply, just nodded, turned, and headed down the hall. The sound of the door being shut and the lock being engaged followed me. Seemed like being away from Black Hawk the last couple of weeks had changed the dynamics. I shrugged the feeling of unease away and walked through the clubhouse and out the door. There was time to worry about that shit later. I was going to my house to grab a few things and head back to Carly's. I needed to apologize for mauling her against the wall after her doctor's appointment. She still needed to take it easy, and I had lost a little of my control. Christ, if I hadn't heard Speed's bike coming down the street, I would have taken her against that damn wall, injured or not. Unacceptable.

I slammed the door after I entered my house with the thought that I needed to kick my own ass because of my behavior. The woman needed to catch up with my feelings for her before I lost the patience I claimed to have.

Chapter Sixteen

Crusher

The sound of a truck pulling up in front of my house had me walking out of the kitchen to the front door, then the sound of Speed's motorcycle had me picking up my pace. I opened the front door and was on the porch before the vehicles were even shut off.

When Carly slid out from the passenger side, I looked her over before I spoke, "What's wrong? Did something happen?" I stood on the porch as Carly made her way to me.

"No, everything's fine." She stepped up on the porch beside me as I watched Sami jump out and wave over her shoulder after handing the keys to the truck to Speed, who was reaching in the back seat. He pulled a bag out and headed in our direction.

"What's going on?" I asked as Speed stepped up on the porch and held the bag and keys out for me to take. When I did, Speed smiled at me, then looked at Carly.

"Yell if you need me, little sis," he said, bent and hugged her before stepping off the porch and walking to his bike.

"I said don't call me that!" Carly yelled, and Speed chuckled.

"Is someone going to tell me what the fuck is going on?" Carly waved at Speed as he headed toward his house, and then she turned and looked up at me with a smile I'd never seen on her face before.

"Let's just say it hit me while you were gone today." She turned and walked into my house. "You coming?" Carly inquired over her shoulder. I followed her in and shut the door, confused about what was happening.

"What hit you?" I stopped and waited for her to turn to look at me.

"That I needed to be home." She shrugged as if it wasn't a big deal that she wanted to go back to Haven. It wasn't going to happen.

"Fuck that. Do you think I am going to take you back to Haven? Seriously?" I tossed her bag, and it landed in the living room. And the woman laughed. My head felt like it was going to explode, and she was laughing. "I'm glad you find this shit goddamn fucking funny."

"When I said I needed to be home, it wasn't Haven I was referring to. It wasn't the house I was staying at in town. Home, Crusher, is where you are, and since you live here, I guess Black Hawk will be where I live, too." I moved toward Carly, picked her up in my arms, and headed for the stairs. "I'll take this as an agreement on your part," she said and wrapped her arms around my neck.

"You better be sure, Carly, because when we enter my bedroom, your future is sealed. There will be no turning back." I stopped at the doorway to give her time to answer. When she bit my chest through my t-shirt, I walked into the room and kicked the door shut behind me.

I know she was expecting me to take her hard. The last few weeks had been leading us to this moment. But not only was she still recovering and needed me to be gentle, but I also needed it that way too.

Carly's body slid down mine as I stood her on her feet, my hands at her waist. I took hold of the bottom of her t-shirt and slowly pushed it up and over her head, revealing the see-through lace bra. Her rosy nipples peaked and showed through her bra cups, begging me to touch them and lick them. She didn't move, but goosebumps formed on her skin as my fingers ran over her collarbone and down the middle of her chest to rest on the hook holding my prize. With a flick, the hook gave way, revealing more than a handful of her perfect breasts.

I leaned down and captured one nipple between my teeth and used my hands to slide the straps off her shoulders and down her arms until the material fell to the floor. Carly

159

arched into me, wanting more, offering everything. Releasing the nipple only to travel my tongue over the peak, circling, and then sucking it into my mouth, rolling the nipple with my tongue. Her moan had my eyes going to hers, only to find her head thrown back and her eyes closed.

"Please, Crusher." At her plea, I released her breast, my hands running down her sides, hooking in the elastic of the tight pants that hugged her body, pushing them down, revealing the creamy white skin beneath. When the material reached her injured thigh, I took great care in moving the material over it. Once cleared, I pushed the pants down to the floor, knelt so she could hold onto my shoulder, and step out of them. With them out of the way, she stood before me in nothing but her panties. I rose, running my hand up the inside of her leg until it reached her apex. The dampness of the panties as my fingers ran from front to back had her placing her forehead on my chest, her warm breath felt through my shirt, and she was panting.

"You're wet for me. I bet if I slide my fingers under the panties, they will slide into your pussy with ease." I moved my hand, and I had been right as my fingers ran through her folds and up into her. I first pumped one finger in and out, then added another, her inner walls closing around them, trying to suck them deeper into her. I twisted my hand slightly and cupped her mound, and curled my fingers to hit the spot that had her breath coming out rapidly and her riding my fingers. "Let go, Carly, cum on my fingers. Give me what I want, baby." I felt her teeth bite down on the skin under my shirt as she bore down on my hand, pushing my fingers deeper. Her scream was muffled against my shirt as her body shook with her release and her juices coated my fingers and hand. Pulling my fingers out and from under her panties, I placed the glistening digits in my mouth and groaned as her sweet but salty taste hit me.

Lifting her up, I laid her on the bed and ripped the panties from her body. When she started recovering from her orgasm, I had my clothes off and a condom laying on the bed.

"Hurry, Crusher," she said, closed her legs, and shifted as if to bring relief. Then she moved to her breasts, and she rubbed, squeezed, and plucked at her nipples. As I watched her, my dick swelled to bursting. Being careful of her leg, I spread her wide and laid down to where my head was between her legs, and I leaned in for the first swipe of my tongue. Fuckin' delicious. My small taste just a minute ago had not done justice. Her pussy was moist, her lips swollen, and her nub was peeking from its hood of protection. The next swipe had her hands reaching for my head. My girl wanted control, wanted my mouth where she needed it the most. Not yet. The bedroom was my domain, she'd take what I gave to her, and she would enjoy it, but it was on my timeframe.

"Don't ever hide what's mine." I lifted her legs over my shoulder, slid my hands under the cheeks of her ass, and shifted while opening her more to me. "Move your hands. Don't try to control me. Relax, and I will give you everything you want and need. When we are in this room, I want to hear you scream my name, Carly, my real name." I placed my lips

161

around her nub and sucked. The move had her pressing her pussy harder against my face. I released the bundle of nerves to run my tongue from back to front. I licked, sucked, and nibbled, then shifted my hands to where my thumbs could reach to spread her lips. I pierced her with my tongue, and I felt her pussy contract around it. I moved it in and out, mimicking what I wanted to do with my dick.

"Crusher, please," she said so breathlessly, and when I pulled away, her hips began to wiggle, and her pussy pushed up, not coming in contact with anything to bring her the relief she was searching for.

"My real name Carly. Give me my real name, and I'll let you orgasm and share in your pleasure as I lap up everything you offer to me." I didn't haven't to wait long.

"Damn it, Russ, let me come!" I bent my head, sucked her clit into my mouth, my right thumb in her pussy, the left one I pressed against her back hole, and her scream echoed in the room as her orgasm rocked her. I pulled my thumb out of her pussy and replaced it with my tongue, lapping up every drop of her cream.

I laid her legs down on the bed on each side of me as I knelt and retrieved the condom, ripping the foil open and rolling it down my length. Carly's body was still shaking when I positioned the head of my cock at her entrance and pushed in. When I bottomed out, I leaned over her and rested my weight on my elbows.

Carly had one arm thrown over her eyes, "Look at me, Carly."

"I don't think I can," was her reply.

"Why can't you look at me?" I would not tolerate her being embarrassed about anything we did in our bedroom together.

"No, I don't think I can have another orgasm." I smiled because her voice sounded more filled with annoyance than it did with denial.

I pulled out and thrust back in, and she moaned, "How about now, think you have another one in you?" She didn't answer as I repeated the movement. I took her moans as my answer and rocked in and out slowly. When I pushed in, my pelvic bone hit just right, placing pressure on her nub.

Pressure from my own orgasm building was bearing down on me, but I needed her to fall over the edge one more time with me. I pulled out, reached between us and thrust back in, hard, and pinched her clit, sending her over with me as I filled the condom with my cum.

I collapsed to the side of her, and we both lay there catching our breaths. I turned and looked at Carly, her eyes closed, her face flushed, her chest rising and falling, and I knew that everything I'd done up to her would be insignificant compared to what we would do together.

Carly snuggled into me and whispered, "I'm tired." I wrapped my arms around her and pulled her close.

Kissing the top of her head, I closed my eyes and listened to her breathing as it changed as she drifted asleep. No matter what happened from now on, knowing that I would end my days like this would be all I needed.

We woke, and though I wanted to roll over and have her again, food was in order. I slid out of bed and watched Carly stretch while pulling on my pants.

"Where are you going?" Her eyes opened and followed my hand as I pulled the zipper up on my jeans.

"Nowhere if I don't get out of the room."

"Then don't go and come back to bed," she said and patted the mattress.

"Food first, and then I will bring you back to the bedroom. There are a lot of things I want to do to you. Some will have to wait until you are completely healed, but I'm sure we can be inventive." I walked to the door, opened it, and entered the hall. "See you downstairs in the kitchen." Her 'you are no fun' had me laughing as I started down the stairs.

Carly appeared in the kitchen just as I finished making the sandwiches. She was dressed, but her hair still held the messiness of having just gotten out of bed. We each had taken several bites of food when my phone beeped. I pulled it out, looked at the screen, and frowned. When I looked up, Carly was staring at me.

"Brax, a woman, and a man are down at the gate demanding to see Stroker or me. Stroker is on his way down. I'm going to go too. You can stay here and finish your sandwich." I rose, and she did too. "Carly, you don't need to go. Sit back down and eat." I started toward the stairs with her on my heels.

"I'm not staying. Though I'm on leave, I am still a deputy with the sheriff's department, and if someone wants to cause trouble, I should be there."

"Fine, I don't have time to argue. Stroker was already on his way." We got fully dressed and in the truck within minutes. As I pulled up behind the parked bikes, I recognized Speed's, Coast's, Devil's, Flirt's, and Jag's—Brax must have called everyone. I looked over at the group of men lined behind Stroker as he and a woman spoke while a man stood by the opened back door of a limo. *What the fuck now?* I thought as I helped Carly out, and we walked toward the crowd. The men parted when they saw me, and as space opened up, my view landed on the woman, her dark brown hair styled pristinely, and the skirt and top looked like the kind women had tailored to fit their form.

I moved beside Stroker, and the woman's attention shifted to me, and a pair of brown eyes looked me over. Fuck me, the woman standing before me had to be my mother because our resemblance could not be denied. She verified my assumption when she spoke.

"Oh my, Russell, you turned into such a handsome man." Marianna smiled hugely at me and started to move in closer.

"What are you doing here, Marianna?" Her smile left, and she frowned at me.

"I am your mother."

"You actually have to earn that title. You, Marianna, were just the woman who carried me. I get it was an accident brought about by another woman's actions. I also know you

165

were going to abort me, but Stroker found out you were carrying his kid and made a deal with you to have me. Something like paying for the rest of your college." Stroker put his hand on my arm. My voice stayed even, but my insides vibrated.

"Stroker, I see you poisoned him against me." I stepped closer to Marianna, and Carly stepped beside me and put her hand in mine. I squeezed her hand but kept my eyes on Marianna.

"Marianna, I told him the truth when he asked about who his mother was." Marianna sneered at Stroker.

"Of course you did," she said to Stroker and turned back to me, "I was eighteen and in college. I wasn't old enough to take on the responsibility of a child. My parents wouldn't have understood and would have made me move home. There is a lot you don't understand, Russell, and won't unless it happens to you." Marianna had the nerve, I'd give her that.

"Get in the car, Marianna, with that dude who I assume is your husband, and go back to DC, and stop calling my phone. It was you, wasn't it?" She nodded her head, and I continued, "If you had spoken and told me who you were, I could have saved you a trip across the country." I was done. I asked about who my mom was when I was thirteen. Stroker told me, and I never asked again. My curiosity was filled.

"Yes, he is my husband, Ron Stetson, the congressman. We'd love to sit down with you and talk and hear about your military service. You did really well in the

Army," she started babbling, and I stared at her. She was only there because of what I had accomplished in the Army.

"Why are you really here, Marianna? Is it me, or what my military career can do for your husband?" A look passed over her face, and I knew I had nailed it.

"Stroker, I'll be up at my house if you need me. I don't have time for this," I said, and Stroker nodded.

"Ron is up for re-election, and yes, your military service record would help greatly. Is that what you want to hear?"

"Marianna, let's just go. It's obvious he doesn't want you here." Ron stepped around the door and put his arm around Marianna's shoulder, she shook him off.

"Look around you, Russell. There is nothing here. Not only would your military record help Ron, but it will also open doors for you in DC. The political parties love a hero. You saved those people in that outside market. Some of the congressmen still talk about it. They want you to come to DC, and if you do, Ron will have their support, not only for re-election but for a few bills he is trying to get passed."

"You know nothing, Marianna! Do you want me to come to DC and talk to your friends about how I obtained that exemplary military record? Let's start with my very first kill shot. I laid on top of a building for fifteen hours, my scope focused on an outdoor market 1600 yards away. Intel had told us it was on a list to be hit because American soldiers had been seen in the area. A ten-year-old boy walked into the market that day. Why did I focus on him? Because it was 125° that day and he was wearing a coat. When he opened it, he was strapped with a bomb that not only would have killed people in the market, it would have taken out half the fucking block. I fired and hit him in the head before he detonated it. Do you know what a .338 fired from an M24 at 1600 yards does to the head? I do. I see it almost every night when I go to sleep because you always remember your first kill. So is that what Ron needs to get re-elected, Marianna?" When she didn't answer and just stared at me, I looked at her husband.

"Take Marianna and leave. Go back to DC, run for president for all I care, just don't contact me again. And, Marianna, I know exactly what I have here. I don't need to look around." Ron turned her toward the opened car door, but Marianna wasn't done yet. She turned back to face me.

"When you are sitting around the club with nothing, just like Stroker and the rest of them, remember I gave you a chance to get out of here," Marianna waved her hand at the dads who stood off to the side, "You enjoy your life, Russell, and your little club. Cutter is the luckiest one of them." Several things happened, she turned back to her husband, I heard Speed's 'what the fuck,' then Carly had let go of my hand and was on Marianna before she could take a step.

"Oh no, you don't!" Carly grabbed Marianna's arm and turned her around to face her. "You don't get to spew shit and walk away." Marianna's eyes went wide, and Ron moved to step between them. I moved to intercept Ron, but there was no need, Carly threw her hand up, and Ron stopped in his tracks. "Don't even fucking think about protecting her now, Congressman Stetson, or I will arrest your ass right here. She started this, and I am going to end it. Then you can take your wife and get the fuck out of this county and state and not return." Ron stepped back, and Carly continued.

"Don't ever talk about my dad, Cutter. You might wear designer suits now, but when the clothes are taken off, there is still a skank underneath. You come in here whining you were young and couldn't raise a child. Well, boo hoo, age didn't keep you from spreading your legs. Then you insult the leadership of this club. Men who have served their country, raised sons, and looked after every member of Black Hawk. Get a fucking clue. That's what family does, bitch. Now get off Black Hawk land, and forget you were here because we will as soon as you leave. Don't come back either, or I will arrest you before you hit the county line."

Speed slapped my back after Carly finished and stepped away from Marianna.

I looked around, and the men's faces held a variation of smiles. My woman just proved that she would stand up for the club she fought against becoming a part of. I felt bad because she should have been home taking care of herself instead of dealing with this. But I would make it up to her.

"Brother, you better not piss her off too bad," Speed said in a low voice as we watched Marianna do exactly what Carly said and get in the car. After the door had swung shut, the driver took off. The man had never gotten out of the car. "And seriously, I will never bitch about Clarice again."

Carly walked toward me, and when she got in reach, I swept her up in my arms and headed to the truck with hoots and whistles sounding behind us.

Once we had gotten back to the house, I sat her on the couch. "We didn't eat much before attending the circus. You want me to grab you something more to eat, baby?"

"No, but I would love to take a bath and soak."

"I think that is a great idea. Come on." I lifted her back up and carried her upstairs.

"Know what would be better than soaking?" she asked, and I shook my head.

"Watersports."

I chuckled, walked into the bedroom, and kicked the door closed behind us. Carly was right. Marianna was already forgotten about.

Chapter Seventeen

Carly

I woke to a hand rubbing over my breasts only to stop and tweak one of my hardened nipples. Even in sleep, my body seemed to respond to him. I wiggled my butt against the cock that was pressed up against me when it hit me.

"How did you get my clothes off without waking me up?" I'd put a t-shirt and shorts on after we came out of the bath, but now I lay naked. Crusher chuckled.

"You sleep like the dead."

"Maybe I was tired. Did you think of that while you were peeling my clothes off?"

"Nope, I woke up cold from where you kicked the covers off us again. I realized I had morning wood when I reached down to pull the covers back up. Didn't want to waste it."

"So you take my clothes—" I didn't finish my sentence because his tongue circled my ear while he lifted my leg, set it on his thigh, and his cock slid between my pussy lips, and the head hit my clit.

When he pulled back and did it again, I didn't care about anything but his hardness inside me. I arched my back, pressing my ass back, giving him better access in the process.

Crusher's tongue made a trail down my neck, and he bit the spot between my shoulder and neck, then he made a trail back up again to circle my ear. The hand on my breast moved to grab my chin, and he turned my head enough to reach my mouth.

His lips met mine, and he bit down on my bottom lip, causing me to gasp, giving him room for his tongue to sweep in. The kiss was consuming me when I felt the head of his cock at my entrance. I broke the kiss.

"Condom," I said before he pushed all the way in. I wasn't on anything.

"I'm clean, babe. I get tested regularly. Plus, I never fucked without a condom, ever. But I want to feel you wrapped around my bare cock." The whole time he talked, he moved his cock back and forth, hitting my clit over and over. I felt myself loosen, my pussy readying itself for what he had to offer.

When I pushed down, the tip of his cock slid in, and I squeezed, pulling a groan from him. It was all the answer he needed as he pushed to the hilt with one thrust of his hips.

The hand that had held my chin splayed out between my hips at my lower stomach, holding me to him as he slid in and out at a relaxed pace.

He moved his hand closer until his middle finger reached my clit, rubbing in slow circles to match the pace he set for my pussy. All the while, he rocked into me and whispered in my ear everything he wanted to do to me, and with each word, my orgasm came closer to the forefront.

"Russ, fuck me!" When I spoke, his hand moved from my clit, and I groaned from the loss of sensation on my clit.

Russ grabbed my hand and placed it where his was before, and with his hand over mine, he moved it back and forth, my own finger rubbing my clit.

"Keep that up, babe, touch yourself." And he lifted his hand from mine only to slide it between us. He pulled out of my pussy and rubbed his cock between my ass cheeks, then he stopped, and I felt the pressure from the head of his cock pressing into my back hole. I shivered and pushed back. "Anyone take your ass before?" he asked as he gathered my cream to apply to my back hole.

"No," was all I got out as he replaced his dick with a finger. I felt the pressure grow as he pushed harder with his finger until he breached the rim. The pleasure and bite of pain combo had me groaning.

"I want to take this ass when we got more time. You gonna let me fuck your ass with my dick, babe?" The few men I had had sex with never talked to me like Crusher did. And I found I liked it a lot. So I knew I would give him anything he asked for, and I pushed back, forcing his finger

173

deeper. "Ah, you like my finger in your ass," then he added a second finger and began rotating them, "you're going to like my cock even more."

"I want your cock in my ass, now, Russ." I began moving my hips, fucking his fingers.

"Goddamn, Carly, hold on." He pulled his fingers out and replaced them with his cock. "Going to be tighter, babe. My cock's a lot bigger than my fingers. And I am gonna tell them it was all your fault if I'm late for Church." My chuckle was cut off when I felt the pressure as he pushed forward; the fullness was like nothing else I had ever experienced as he became fully seated. He held still while I tried to adjust until he couldn't take it anymore, and neither could I. "Gotta fuckin' move now."

He splayed his hand between my hipbones to hold me in place as he pulled out and slammed back in. "Fuckin' not going to last much longer." The hand on my stomach moved down until he cupped my pussy, slid two fingers in, and set a rhythm, fucking both my holes. The dual sensations had goosebumps forming on my skin, and when he pushed the heel of his hand against my clit, I threw my head back on his shoulder and screamed his name as my orgasm racked my body.

Crusher had pumped a few more times before I felt the warmth of his cum as it coated the inside of my ass. He continued to pump his fingers in and out until I rode the last wave of my orgasm.

"Worth being late," Crusher said, leaned over me and kissed my forehead, then pulled back, looking me in the eye.

"Love you, Carly. And I hate that I just told you that and have to leave for Church. After the cookout later, I will make it up to you. I promise."

"I'll hold you to that. I love you, too, Russ." I wrapped my arms around him, and he kissed me.

When he pulled away, got out of bed, and looked down at me, he groaned, "Worst possible time." Then walked into the bathroom. It didn't take him long to shower and get dressed. I would help the women of the club set up for the cookout that was scheduled for after Church.

"See you when I get back, baby." Crusher leaned down and kissed me, then out the door he went. I lay in bed and listened as the front door opened, then I sat up only to fall back on the bed again when I heard Devil shout, "Might want to close your bedroom window the next time, brother."

I didn't hear Crusher's response because I covered my head with the pillow. No more nighttime fresh air for me.

With Crusher gone to Church, I showered, dressed in my last clean clothes, and ate. I had just finished putting my plate and glass in the dishwasher when I heard the knock. When I answered the door, Sami and Ally stood on the porch.

"You ready to go help set up for the cookout, Aunt Carly?" Ally walked in, and Sami followed.

"I thought we could take the car because I have a few things to carry over. Did you want to ride with us instead of walking?" I needed to go to town and grab some more of my clothes at the other house.

Last night as Crusher and I lay in bed, we discussed my moving in. Since I still couldn't lift anything heavy, Crusher said he would have the others help him this coming week. Still didn't help with my clothing problem right now.

"How about I drive, and I will drop you off and run to the other house? I'm out of clothes. What I'm wearing is the last." I grabbed the keys off the table in the hall as I spoke.

"Why don't you just wash what you have here?" Sami asked, and I could do that, but I only had one other set. Two outfits weren't going to cut it. Plus, Crusher told me my revolver was in my closet locked in its case, and I wanted to grab that too.

"I won't be gone long, and I didn't make anything for the cookout. So I think I'll swing by the bakery and pick something up." Ally jumped up and down and put in her order for cupcakes.

"Okay, but don't be too long. I don't think the guys will be at Church that much longer. You might pass them on the road to town." We walked out and headed for Crusher's truck. I needed to bring my truck and bike to Black Hawk.

After a stop in front of Speed's and Sami's place, we pulled up beside the clubhouse, and I helped Sami and Ally carry things into the kitchen. Several women greeted me and introduced themselves. This was just to be a club cookout because the children would be attending, which I couldn't say I wasn't happy about not having to watch the hang-arounds all over the men. I hadn't had to face that yet with Black Hawk, and if they were anything like the ones who hung around Haven, they didn't give a shit if the man was taken. Made for some interesting parties when the ol' ladies were around.

We spoke for a few minutes, then I told Sami and the ladies that I wouldn't be long. I wanted to be back before Crusher because I didn't want to listen to him complain about my driving or the nine hundred other reasons he would come up with.

I waved at the man at the gate and then turned on the main road into town. As I drove past Soft Tails, I noticed the parking lot was full, which meant Church was still in progress. If I hurried, I would make it back in plenty of time.

Sue was outside when I pulled up, putting a few things in her car. "Hey, Sue, you going to the cookout?" I yelled to her.

"Yeah, Stroker called and invited me. I haven't spent a lot of time there since Wolf passed. Even Shakes and a few other of the ol' ladies I'm friends with called to tell me to come. Aren't you going to be there? I can't believe that man of yours would let you skip it." It seemed news had traveled fast through the club.

"Just grabbing a few things from inside, then I'm heading back. They were still at Soft Tails when I passed by." I unlocked the door and opened it, then turned back to Sue. "I'll talk with you some more at the club."

"Sure thing, I'm heading there now. Got some of the things they're going need to set up before that hungry bunch shows up. Good to see you're getting back to yourself." Sue waved and got in her car, and I walked into the house, shutting the door behind me.

After I had gotten upstairs, I grabbed a couple of small tote bags, gathered a few articles of clothing, and shoved them in the bags. Next, I took my service revolver and placed the box on top of them. I looked around the bathroom for anything I might need until my stuff was packed once again and moved to Crusher's house.

I walked down the stairs, set the bags by the door, and headed to the kitchen. I didn't know if anyone else drank wine, but I had a few bottles I kept around for when I wanted a glass. Which wasn't often, considering I preferred beer.

When I retrieved the bottles from the top shelve of the cabinet, I turned and then stopped dead in my tracks.

"What the fuck are you doing here?"

"Hello, *daughter*," Stone sneered.

Chapter Eighteen

Crusher

When we pulled up to Soft Tails, the lot was already full. I knew we weren't early, but we weren't late either. Fuck, this was not going to be good.

"Shit, when Roscoe beats us here, you know you're late." Speed shook his head and walked toward the door. "Now we are probably going to have to listen while the dads bitch us out in front of the whole club."

"Bullshit, I'm not getting yelled at, Crusher, because you were too busy getting your dick wet this morning," Flirt followed behind Speed, griping.

"I didn't ask you fuckers to wait on me. You could have left. I'm a big boy, could have found my way here on my own. Besides, we are on fucking time, assholes. Unless the time was changed and no one told us." I walked beside Devil as we were the last to get off our bikes.

"I haven't seen Dad for a couple of days. They'd been holed up in the office working on what, I have no idea. I asked, and he told me not to worry about it, that they had it handled," Devil said.

"I got told the same shit by Prez," I said, and as Speed pulled open the door, Tank and Dare were standing there.

"Hey, brothers," Speed said and held out his hand. We all watched as Dare and Tank both looked down at his hand but neither extended theirs. The look on their faces was blank and detached. "What the fuck is going on?"

"Prez will tell you, boys. Go take a seat, you are the last to get here." Tank stepped between us and threw the lock on the door. I looked around the room that now held chairs facing a long table where the leadership sat. At the table sat Stroker, Preacher, Romeo, Flyboy, and even Cruz, Coast's dad, who usually stood off to the side since he was an enforcer.

We walked to the front to take a seat. Speed went to sit with the dads since he'd already taken Cutter's position.

"Speed, you can sit with the others," Stroker looked at Speed when he spoke and motioned to the empty seat beside me. It didn't escape me how quiet the room was. Speed stood beside the table where the dads were sitting and looked at each one. The only one that looked back at him was Stroker.

Stroker cocked his eyebrow at Speed, "You got a problem with what I said, Speed?"

Speed's lips thinned, and he glared back. A few seconds passed with the stare down until finally, Speed was the one to break it as he turned toward me and the others, "Nah, Prez, your meeting, you run it how you like." Speed sat down beside me. I looked back at the Prez and the others, and they were looking at us. Their faces were the same as Tank's and Dare's: blank, distant.

Fuck me, Jag was right; not calling them until after we had things handled with Carly had pissed them off. I didn't want to have a yelling match in front of the entire club, but how we were being treated pissed me off.

"Anybody else feel as though we went back in time like twenty years?" Flirt leaned over and said, and Romeo's head snapped in his direction.

"Watch your mouth and show respect in here or get out," Romeo said as he looked at Flirt. If this meeting didn't start soon, there was going to be a fight. I could feel the tension in the room, and the only sound was that of members shifting in their seats behind us.

Flirt was right, though; it did feel like we went back twenty years to us sitting in that office at Black Hawk because of some dumbass shit young boys do, waiting to get yelled at and to find out what our punishment would be.

"Okay, let's get this meeting underway. We got a lot of shit that needs to be covered. Romeo, you start with the financials."

At Stroker's words Romeo opened the folder in front of him. "As of today, every business owned and run by Black Hawk members shows a profit. With the exception of Custom Rides. The profit margin is showing a steady increase every month, if this continues at the end of next year, Black Hawk will have doubled across the board." Romeo, the treasurer of the club, continued on with each individual business's profit. This whole meeting was strange because the profit and loss sheets were something the club only went over at the end of each year. We weren't even halfway through the current year.

"Thanks, Romeo," Stroker said and looked over at Cruz. "Cruz, you want to address any problems going on internally that the club needs to handle."

Cruz, enforcer for the club, opened the folder in front of him, "Just a couple, Prez. Boss and Turk have been warned twice for fighting with each other over the last of the marijuana plants that are ready for harvest. Seems they didn't want to give that part of the business up to go legal. I've spoken with both men, and they've agreed to stop fighting with each other and work together. Flyboy got the plant problem solved." Cruz looked out at the members, "You agreed with the assessment, Boss? Turk?" I looked over my shoulder to see Boss and Turk sitting beside each other in the back.

"Agreed, Cruz," both men said at the same time. Boss and Turk were real brothers on top of being Black Hawk brothers. When they weren't fighting each other, you started asking if hell froze over. If that was the only internal issue in the club, everyone was doing what they were supposed to. "The last thing, which is new and hasn't been addressed, is a situation with the ex-VP of Haven, one that has seemed to have made its way to Black Hawk. The problem arising from this is that a few of the current members and one of the leadership have forgotten that everything that goes on in a club comes through the chain of command and, lastly, to the Prez. They are to be involved first before any decision-making is held. Those members broke that process, and recommendation on how to deal with them needs to be addressed."

"Thanks, Cruz. We will move on to Flyboy and Preacher. Gentlemen, you can start when you are ready."

Preacher, the club secretary, opened the folder in front of him and flipped through several pieces. I sat, lost, listening to them go over each thing dealing with the club. I turned and looked at my friends, and their faces reflected what had to be on mine. What the fuck? And the part that pissed me off most was saving the reprimanding till the end. Like there should be any, we handled the issue and reported when it was over. Not like we hid shit from any of them. Never have we been reprimanded in front of the entire club; it was usually handled in the Prez's office. Well, I would sit here and listen to their shit, and if they wanted to do it in front of the whole club, I would voice our side in front of the whole club too. I just wished they would speed it up, I wanted to get back to Carly. I didn't want her sitting at the cookout with a bunch of women she hadn't met. I wanted to be able to introduce her so she would feel comfortable and not overwhelmed.

Preacher pulled out a paper and sat it on top, "The records are up-to-date on every ride we have done for the charities Black Hawk contributes to. We have two we schedule every year, and the funds we make go a long way in helping these groups. The Boys Ranch and the Girls Ranch provide an opportunity for kids who have lost their way to get on the right track again. When the one for the Boys Ranch is held, it is only the men who participate in the ride. The Girls Ranch ride includes the women of the club because they run that one, but since most of the ol' ladies don't ride their own bikes, the Black Hawk men join in on it. We expect the same turnout and fund goal for this year." Preacher looked over at Flyboy.

Flyboy, the VP, was the only one who didn't open the file in front of him, and thank God, the fucker was full and had to be a couple of inches thick. We'd be in Church until next week if he went over each.

"The newest thing is filed and ready to be operational if the plants Cruz told us about meet the specifications. I made several calls to the government, and I got it approved that Boss and Turk can continue to grow marijuana for medicinal purposes. We had to jump through a few hoops and call in a few markers, but it went through. A few guidelines will have to be followed, and Boss and Turk have those. We should be in compliance within two months.

"I have all the paperwork ready with the changes that are required for the Black Hawk Corp and its subsidiaries.

The forms just need to be notarized and filed in the courts by an attorney. That finishes my part, Prez." Flyboy looked over at Stroker, who stood and then looked at me and slid his eyes over the others. It was time for us, I guessed.

"Crusher, Speed, Coast, Devil, Flirt, and Jag sit in front of us today for not informing the club of an issue until it was partially settled. With that being said, I would like to cover a little of what these members have done for this club. They have never failed to support any member who needed something taken care of or just someone to talk with. From putting a roof on the garage to repairing Soft Tails every other weekend when it would get trashed inside from fights. In that aspect, they have been the perfect members.

"Now, as a dad to one of these gentlemen, I would like to speak to this club. Me and the gentlemen beside me, including the empty chair to represent Cutter, raised these six, but not alone. They were raised within Black Hawk, with every member playing a part. And at times, they were thorns in the same members' sides with the mischief that young boys can get into. We celebrated achievements with them, we even cried as a club when they were given a choice to leave so they could experience the world to see if this is where they wanted to be, and they took it. Not one member voiced their concern as each year passed by, and they continued to stay away, making their homes elsewhere.

"They came back one by one to Black Hawk, and as their parents, we had hopes they would take over this club in time after learning how the inner dealings of it worked."

Stroker stopped and picked up the glass of water in front of him and took a drink.

I don't know how the others felt about what Stroker was saying, but the quiver in his voice that I picked up on shook me. It was like a father pleading his son's case before a jury. For a brief second, the thought of what I would do without this club had me sick to my stomach. This was home, and no matter where I was sent in the military, Black Hawk was the one thing I knew that would still be here when I came back. Stroker looked out at the members again.

"As parents, we wanted them to succeed and hoped they took our teachings to heart and could run Black Hawk like us. Speed in his short time back, filled Cutter's position already. Son, know your dad is here in spirit participating in this." Stroker turned to the others who stood, putting each of them shoulder to shoulder. I imagine as young men in the military, they were intimidating.

"What they have done is surpass us at every turn. From the young men who left for their own adventures in life to the men who sit in front of us now—they have proven they are ready to take Black Hawk over and keep it thriving into the future. So as President of Black Hawk and my last order of business and with the unanimous member votes—I turn this club over to my son, Russell "Crusher" Davis, Black Hawk's new president, and his fellow leaders. May their reign be as enjoyable as ours." Stroker smiled and held out the patch to me. I stood and walked to him, taking the patch in my hand and looking down at it.

To say I was speechless would be an understatement. I looked over my shoulder at my friends and smiled. In a way, we had spent our entire lives preparing for this moment. I looked back at Stroker, it couldn't have been easy on him or the other dads to deal with six boys, and yet, they'd done it, not once complaining. I couldn't have picked a better dad even if I had been given a choice. I grabbed him by the shoulders and pulled him into a hug, I owed this man a lot, and I loved him more than I could express with words.

No one had yet spoken or made a sound. Stroker stepped back after I released him. "Well, Prez, you might want to have the others hand their patches over and then maybe end this meeting so we can have a drink and attend that celebration cookout the women are putting together."

I turned to the other dads with grins splitting their faces. "Enjoy retirement, gentlemen, and know your legacy is in good hands." Preacher, Romeo, Cruz, and Flyboy held out the patches for their sons to take from them. The exchange was made, and I faced the club for the first time as its president.

"We'd like to thank you for your trust, your loyalty, and most importantly, your friendships. Now let's end this meeting and fucking celebrate." The men stood, and the club exploded with noise. We were hugged and slapped on the back, so many times I would have sworn something was going to get knocked loose inside me.

"Holy shit, when that started, I thought we were done," Jag said as he walked up beside me. We'd finally caught a break with the congratulations. Our dads joined the other members in a toast for all their years taking care of them. Each of us would talk with our dad later. That would be the father/son private moment on what took place today.

"I know, I thought you were right, and we pissed them off. Was worried there a second that we were getting kicked out." I shook my head. They'd pulled off a good one. None of us had had a clue.

"That shit was so fucked up." Coast walked up to join Jag and me. Speed, Flirt, and Devil walked toward us.

"Did you ever think this day was actually going to come? I thought for sure they would drag it out," Flirt said.

"Me, too," Devil said.

"You don't know how close I came to ripping my fuckin' patch off when that shit started. The only thing that kept me from doing it is the respect I have for them," Speed said.

We talked with members and shook hands until the only ones left in Soft Tails were the five dads and us. At the bar, shots were poured, and with a toast for the future, the shots were thrown back. Stroker's phone rang just as we set the shot glasses back on the bar.

It couldn't be good, and I sure as fuck hoped it wasn't the sheriff calling because someone wrecked. But while he listened to the caller, his eyes met mine.

"Yeah, we are still here. Got it covered, Sue. Uh huh, stay in your house. We will be there in less than five. Don't do anything to bring notice to yourself," Stroker advised, then disconnected the call.

"Stone and his buddy are in town. They are held up in Sami's old place," he paused, and my stomach dropped.

No fucking way, I left her in bed. She was going to help Sami, so there was no way she was there. But my gut wasn't in agreement.

"Sue was leaving for the cookout while Carly was arriving. They spoke for a few minutes, Carly went in, and Sue left for the clubhouse.

"Sue had gotten halfway to the club and remembered the potato salad. When she returned and walked to the kitchen, she noticed two men entering the house. Crusher, Carly is in the house with them."

Fuuuck! I was going to need to focus if I was going to get to her. I just claimed her. No way I was going to lose her now.

"I going to kill that fucker with my bare hands!" Speed yelled.

The others moved in. "We need a plan of action. And, Dad, I hope you have the keys on you." Soft Tails was club owned, and all our businesses had a few surprises in the structure because you never knew when you would need something.

Cruz stepped around the bar, and with the key in hand, he stuck it in the lock that was hidden by a small picture on the wall. When he turned it, the wall of booze slid to the side, and the guns were displayed.

We talked about how we would handle the issue while we got what we needed from the wall and the ammo to go with it.

Speed even called Wild Bill, and told him we were going after Stone and Jacks, who we suspected was the other man. They talked for a few minutes, and then Speed hung up.

"Wild Bill's men are on their way down for pick up. Said he'd appreciate it if they were alive but would understand if they weren't. You going to be alright to do this, brother?" Speed waited for my reply.

"You bet your ass. Let's go get my woman." I didn't wait for any response. I turned and headed toward the door. Stone and his buddy were going to regret coming out of hiding.

Chapter Nineteen

Carly

The man that stood in the kitchen, whom I hadn't seen in over five years, hadn't aged well. Grey had taken over most of his brown hair. His face was ruddy, and his eyes were sunken with circles around them. Evidently, being on the run had taken its toll. His body looked in no better shape, he lost the muscles he once had in abundance, and his clothes hung on the smaller frame.

I might have cowed in front of him at one time, but now, not so much. I'd grown up, came into my own, and left everything to do with him behind me.

"Got nothing to say, little girl?" When he opened his mouth to talk, his teeth showed the years of drinking and of tweaking.

"Yeah, I got plenty to say. You made the wrong move today. You always boasted about how smart you are. That no one could get anything over on you. Your ass was stupid then, and what little you might have had, by the looks of you, you drank that away," I said before my mouth was going to get me in to a shit ton of trouble as he moved toward me and slapped me across my face. The slap stung, but I wouldn't let him have even that on me.

"You watch your goddamn mouth. You look like that cunt of a mother when I met her. And you are no better either. I've seen you, you fucking the biker from Black Hawk. You think he's going to make you his ol' lady because you spread your legs. Your mother tried for years to get that fucker to make her his, and all he did was keep knocking her up. Took the one kid from her so she ran so he couldn't get you. He knew she was pregnant, he just didn't want you. Hell, no one does.

"Now get your scrawny ass into the living room. Wild Bill always did like you, and since I couldn't get to the princess and that little heathen, you are the next best thing. Killing you will be just as good as them. Black Hawk will mourn, and so will Haven, leaving both of the clubs weak. But I'm counting on that they'll blame each other, and while they are fighting, the few men still loyal to me will set about taking over Haven. That damn club was meant to be mine."

Jacks grabbed my arm, and when he shoved me into the chair, his hand moved over my breast and squeezed. "Gonna have a little fun with you before I kill you." He stepped back, and I kicked my leg out, catching his knee and causing it to buckle under him. He stood and backhanded my other cheek with such force my head jerked to the side.

"Quit fucking around, Jacks, and look for shit we can pawn. Going to need some cash when it's time to move on Haven."

"Haven is going to take you down, and I can only imagine what Shock and Freak will think up for you."

"Shut the fuck up. You don't know dick. Those fuckers couldn't find me in almost six years," he sneered.

"Wrong there too, asswipe. They will come for you. They didn't find you before because they didn't lift the right rock." They had to be getting out of Church. Crusher would go to the cookout, and Sami would tell him where I was. Or even Sue would. I just had to buy some time.

"Go into the kitchen and see if you can find a towel and some tape. Her ass needs gagged." He walked over and stood in front of Jacks and me as he headed toward the kitchen. He took the back of his hand and ran it down my cheek. "You look just like her, I think I might join Jacks in the fun, see if you fuck as good as her. I'll give the cunt that. She was game for anything. Promise her a tweak, and I could line guys up, charge them twenty dollars, and Clarice would fuck and suck. Made good money on her in her younger days. Hell, maybe I should just take you and put you to work making me some money. What ya think?"

I would not let this asshole get to me.

"I think you are a sick fucker who has penis envy. Don't forget I've seen your dick, it's small." Just as he reared back to slap me again, a huge crash echoed through the house. I heard Jacks' screams of pain as Stone grabbed my arm and yanked me up in front of him just as Speed walked through the now busted front door.

"Hey, little sis. Heard you needed some help." Speed smiled and winked at me, then frowned as he moved closer. "You hit her, motherfucker? I'll be sure to tell Wild Bill that, see what his boys can do for you. You might be going back alone if your buddy bleeds out. Well, either way, it depends if he is breathing when they load him up."

Coast came into view and moved to stand beside Speed, blood splattered over the front of his shirt.

"One down. Goddamn, that son-of-a-bitch is good," Coast said as he looked around, I presumed to take in the situation. And what the fuck was up with being so nonchalant while I have a fucking gun jammed in my back and Stone's nasty arm around my neck half choking me.

"Don't move any closer, you pricks or I will kill her."

I swear bikers are all freakin' nuts as Speed moved over to the chair and plopped down like he was there for a damn visit.

"Instead, why don't we have a little chat before we kill you?"

What the hell? Chat? And where is Crusher?

"What, you want to chat? How about chatting about how I killed your dumbass daddy, boy? Or do you want to know how easy your mother died?" The blue in Speed's eyes darkened as he stood at the mention of Cutter. Stone was stupider than I thought. He might kill me, but Speed would be on him as soon as the trigger was pulled.

"Got your attention now, don't I? Clarice was easy. A little extra in her needle, and she didn't even last long enough to enjoy the high. Now Cutter, well, I hadn't planned to kill him. I was just going to share the information Clarice had told me about Carly being Cutter's kid for a price. Kept that information when she told me. I'd already raised the brat as mine. Then the whore gets mad one night when I won't give her a hit. Throws a hissy fit and blurts out she was going to leave me, take her daughter to her real father, and he would give her money, and she would buy her own shit." Speed said nothing, but Coast moved closer while Stone was busy spewing his shit.

"So you killed Clarice, that supposed to scare us? Or do you think that shit is going to upset me? I didn't know the bitch." Speed's eyes never left Stone, he just kept getting him to talk. I noticed that Stone moved us every time Speed or Coast shifted.

"Now Cutter, I needed money, and he had it. Creeper snuck on the property at Black Hawk and left the note for Cutter. We knew he would head to town, if for nothing else, just to see what I was up to. Waited for the bastard on the road, he came around the corner, and we were sitting, lined across the road, and he lost control. He hit pretty hard, but it didn't kill him. I did lean down and tell him about Carly. I would have let him live, but he spit in my face, so it was easy just to grab his neck, and with a twist, it was done." God, I lived with this man, called him dad, and he spoke of killing as if you would talk about what was for dinner.

Stone shifted to get us out of both men's reach again. Coast took a big step to the side, putting him in arm's reach of us. Stone moved the gun from my back to point it at Coast, Speed tore me out of Stone's grip and dropped us to the ground, and I heard glass break, then Stone screamed and fell to the ground, blood pouring from the hole in his shoulder.

"You okay?" Speed asked as he pulled us to our feet. I looked over at Stone as Coast was securing him. The room filled with men in seconds after Stone's scream, but none of them was Crusher. I didn't know how to feel: disappointed, hurt, I couldn't pick one.

"I'm fine. They just slapped me a couple of times because I was giving them shit," I said as arms wrapped around me from behind.

"No, not you, baby." I turned at the voice and found myself in Crusher's arms.

"It was you, you shot Stone through the window. Speed and Coast aren't crazy, they were just corralling him so he would move where you could see him."

"Now, baby, I wouldn't go that far." He kissed the top of my head, then looked at me. "What are you doing here anyway? You should have been at Black Hawk. You shouldn't even be driving." Good Lord, how my life had changed. I patted his chest, and that's when I saw it.

"You have a president patch pinned on you."

"Baby, they usually give you a patch when you become the president," Crusher said and moved us out of the way as they brought a gagged Jacks out of the kitchen to sit him beside Stone.

"Did the dads really step down, Crusher? Sami said you guys were supposed to take over, but no one thought they would actually do it." Crusher started toward the front door, he moved us outside while Speed and Coast were talking into phones, and Devil was patching Jacks and Stone to keep them from bleeding on everything.

"The dads turned it all over. That's why we were still in town when the call came in from Sue. She had to come back to her house because she forgot something for the cookout and saw the men come in. That's where I was at, Carly, at Sue's house watching through the scope on my rifle, waiting to get my shots off. Wild Bill's guys are on their way to pick these two up. And I am taking you home." He led me to my truck. "You okay to drive, baby?" I kissed his lips.

"The others will wait for Haven and fix the doors while they are here. Let's get you home. We have a cookout to go to, but I want to love on my woman because I had the shit scared out of me today." He leaned down and rested his forehead on mine.

"He killed my mother and my father, Crusher. He cheated me out of a dad. They both did."

"I'm sorry, baby. You didn't deserve any of that shit. If I could change any of it for you, I would."

"I know you would, Crusher. I'm sorry you had to stop your celebration for this crap. Not every day you get a club turned over to you." And I was sorry, for him, for the others too. Instead of saving me once again, they should be celebrating with their brothers.

"I love you, baby."

"Thanks for coming for me today. I love you so much, Crusher."

"Baby, no matter what. I will always come for you. Let's go home, Carly. I'll be right behind you if you are sure about driving." Crusher stepped back and opened the truck door for me. I went to get in and paused, looking over my shoulder at him.

"I'm good. But, Crusher, I'm not calling you Prez." He helped me up into the seat, chuckling.

"Wouldn't expect it from you, baby." Crusher leaned in and kissed me.

My life might not have always been roses, but I wouldn't have changed a thing because it was what brought Crusher to me. And even kissing me in a truck parked on the side of the road—he felt like home, and for the first time, I couldn't wait to see what the future held for me—for us.

Epilogue

Devil

"Why did we bring the truck, Uncle Devil? I wanted to ride on the back of your bike."

This had to be the longest fifteen-minute drive in history. Whatever possessed me to volunteer to do this needed to be exorcised right out of me.

"Spider, your mom doesn't want you riding on the back of our bikes yet. Besides, we are going to the bakery and need the space to put the goodies. We can't shove them in the saddlebags, can we?"

"No, I don't like my cupcakes with smushed icing."

"Who does?"

"Who does what?" she asked.

"No, sweetheart, 'who does' is just a phrase... Never mind, we're almost there." I was going back to Black Hawk, hiding in the garage, and keeping my mouth shut when the women were around. It never failed that one of us got suckered into doing something. Speed and Crusher probably high-fived when I said I would do this.

Sami had invited everyone for dinner. She and Carly were cooking for all the help we gave in moving them in, then they realized there was nothing for dessert. I should have known I was being set up when their own men didn't say one damn word. Couldn't wait to see what the others got talked into for their parts in the Ally turned shyster role. Because damn, I knew we all had foul mouths, but who knew they were that bad. Sami evidently did now since we had to come clean when she found the shoebox in Ally's closet full of dollar bills. After Sami counted it, Spider/Shyster, as some had begun to call her, had made a hundred and two dollars in just over a week. Combine that with what I like to refer to as 'the oil incident' did not help our cause. So trying to get back in the woman's good graces, I asked if they needed anything, and before I knew it, I'm in the truck on my way to the bakery in town.

Of course, when you mention the bakery within a mile of Ally, you're buying cupcakes, and she's in the truck with you because she wants to pick them out. That part I didn't mind because Ally's a sweetheart. Besides, she never fails to make me laugh with the things her little girl brain comes up with.

"You are grouchy. Maybe you need laid, Uncle Devil." I almost wrecked the truck when I jerked my head around to look over my shoulder at Ally in the backseat.

"Where did you hear that?" Okay, we were going to have to be more diligent around the club if she heard shit like that. Sami would have all our balls instead of just Speed's if she heard Ally say that.

"I heard Daddy tell Momma that she was grouchy and needed to be laid. When I'm grouchy, am I going to need to be laid, too?" I glanced in Ally's direction after I parked in front of the bakery. She wore a frown on her face as if in thought. And no, I was not going to go there. However, I wasn't against a little payback. Especially since Sami really couldn't come after us for what Ally heard from her dad.

I got out and went around the front of the vehicle to open the door, so Ally could get out. "Sweetheart, why don't you ask your daddy that question during dinner tonight? I bet he can answer it way better than I can."

All of a sudden, I was looking forward to dinner. Who said karma didn't have a sense of humor?

"'K, but I hope I like being laid."

Yeah, it might be wrong, but I was going to deflect. I didn't want to think of her grown and getting anything from a damn man.

"Let's see about getting you some cupcakes." Ally immediately grabbed my hand, and we walked to the door, and then she pushed it open, dragging me behind her. No one stood between her and cupcakes.

I looked around. I hadn't been in the bakery since before I left for the military. We stood in line behind several customers as Bailey darted behind the counter, filling their orders.

As I watched her, the girl who had at one time told me she loved me would feel the same if she knew the truth.

That I was responsible for her brother's death.

Acknowledgments

My thanks are for the readers who gave a new author a try and enjoyed the first book enough to come back. In everyday life spare time is hard to come by, so for you to spend what little time you have to read my books, is an honor I hope to never take for granted.

Thanks again and enjoy your reading.

Carson

About the Author

Carson Mackenzie enjoys writing romance with a real feel inside the stories. She writes with the belief not every man is a jerk and not every woman needs saving.

Carson lives in the South with one of her sons, a Great Dane and two adopted shelter dogs that keep the household in line. Books have always been a part of her life. There is nothing better to her than curling up and relaxing with a good story and losing herself in someone else's world for a few hours.

Writing stories and growing as an author with each book is her goal. She wants to reach the level where a reader knows when they see her name, they can trust in the fact there will be a good story as they flip through the pages.

Carson's been her writing journey for a few years. As she's finally starting to settle in, her only regret is she hadn't started sooner.

To stay up to date with Carson – visit her website- https://carsonmackenzieauthor.com/ or sign up for her newsletter- https://landing.mailerlite.com/webforms/landing/l2k1l8.

Books by Carson Mackenzie

Black Hawk MC

Speed
Crusher
Devil
Ghost
Jag
Coast
Flirt

Haven MC

Moose's Regret

Hawk's Bounty
Keg's Revelation

Desert Phoenix MC

Desert Phoenix Rising

Standalones

Her Way or No Way
two paths One destiny

Boxed Sets

Black Hawk MC Books 1-3
Black Hawk MC Books 4-7
Haven MC Books 1-3